A SINISTER SPELL IN
FAERYWOOD FALLS

BLYTHE BAKER

∾

Living under an evil curse is bad ... but dying under one is worse.

Marianne Huffler is cursed – and not just with the ghastly middle name of Prudence. Until she can figure out the magic secrets of her past, she's doomed to suffer permanent bad luck – and the occasional attempt on her life.

Leaving her hometown of Hillbilly Hollow, Marianne travels to the mountains of Colorado, where she hopes to find answers. What she doesn't expect to find? Dead bodies!

But when corpses start popping up, Marianne gets drawn into investigating the mysterious deaths. With a cunning vampire, a good looking werewolf, and an angry spell weaver among the suspects, can Marianne catch a killer ... before the killer catches *her*?

∾

1

There was no sound except for the pounding of blood rushing through my ears. The air was stale and heavy, with particles of dust swirling, thick with ancient smoke. It coated the inside of my lungs like tar, clogging my sinuses and causing me to sputter and cough.

At least, it would have...if I could open my mouth at all.

Veiled darkness pressed in on my eyes, as if stretched across my face, attempting to blind me. I pried my eyelids open, willing them to catch a glimpse of any light, no matter how small.

Distant, echoing shouts made me stumble, stretching out my hands in front of me. My palms scraped against splintery boards and hot, sticky pain ran between my fingers.

"Ma...rianne..."

The voice was faint, as if it were navigating its way through a dense forest.

A light flared into life, revealing itself at the end of an old, narrow wooden corridor. It wavered and dimmed, and for a brief moment, I feared the light would disappear or that it never existed in the first place.

I dragged my leaden legs toward the light, willing them to move. I couldn't stop. I had to reach that light, somehow, some way.

"Ma...rianne..."

I knew that voice. Only one person ever called me by my middle name of Marianne. To everybody else, I had always been Prudence. The pounding in my ears grew louder, rushing to remind me that I was living. Each beat of my heart was a reminder that I was still breathing.

My hands struck something hard and splintery. An old wooden door had appeared in my path, blocking the light. It was fastened with iron brackets and hinges, and the doorknob was imperfectly round. I grabbed it with tacky hands, and shoved my full weight against it.

I stumbled through the doorway and into a wide, shadowed room. Starlight streamed through a nearby window that revealed the night sky outside.

As I looked around, I realized I was in an old western-style fort. It was just how I remembered it, aside from the wavering colors and the haze only a few feet in front of me. Out the window, I could still see the canons in the yard. Inside, golden plaques adorned the walls, describing the surroundings for visitors.

A museum fixed forever in time, putting an old fort like this on pause. We had to cling to our past. We had to know it. We had to learn it and discover it. Without our pasts, we had no future.

As I looked to the sky out the window, it began to shrink, as if it was falling down toward me, and one by one, the stars began winking out of existence.

My heart raced. Where were they going? Didn't they know I needed them? I couldn't survive without them –

My foot struck something. I looked down. The floorboards were wide and even. I recognized them. But that wasn't all I found. There was a man. A young man, really. He had a smooth complexion, with dark hair and brilliant green eyes that were turned toward the window, gazing out at the stars that weren't there anymore.

"Ma...rianne..."

It was his voice. I knew it was. But his mouth didn't move.

As I knelt down to touch his face, the tears falling from my eyes drenched the front of his jacket. Dark, swirling bruises coated his neck, like fingers stained in juices from autumn's first blackberries.

His skin was as cold as the floor on which he was stretched out. The only light in his eyes was a reflection of the moon outside, which was shrinking like a dissolving mint.

Shadows rushed over him, a tidal wave of gloom. My fingers grasped at emptiness, striking the floorboards instead of cold flesh.

No...

I SCREAMED and opened my eyes. A horn blared, and I gasped, my heart leaping into my throat.

Brilliant amber sunlight stung my eyes as I squinted against the sudden brightness. But it wasn't just the sun. Two other orbs of light, tinted with blue, were shining in front of me.

My fingers tightened around the dense foam of the

steering wheel I was gripping, and I yanked it to the side, veering out of the way of the bright blue lights.

Panting, I eased my foot off the gas, and grasped at my chest with one hand.

I'd dozed off like an idiot and swerved into the other lane of traffic.

My fingers trembling, I pulled my car off the side of the road. I put it in park and smashed the hazards button before letting my head fall into my hands.

I could have died. Even if that other car hadn't been coming, I could have gone off the road, hit a tree, toppled over a cliff...

I focused on my breathing, trying to will myself to calm down. I took several deep, long breaths, holding them like my therapist had taught me to before releasing them.

It was only a dream. A dream that I definitely shouldn't have been having while I was *driving*, but it wasn't any more than that.

Not only that, but it was a dream I'd had way too many times.

It was always the same. It was dark, and I was terrified. I would wander along until I'd find my way into the big room. I knew that place in the dream, an old 19th century western fort in my hometown. It had been converted to a museum long ago. It was a place that I'd been to on field trips as a little girl, where volunteers from the local historical society always held an amazing fall festival every year, complete with a haunted tour of the fort where people would dress up and try to scare visitors.

But it wasn't the fort that was so confusing. It was the man I inevitably found at the end. I always hoped I'd wake up before that part.

The man's name was Jacob. I had loved him.

And he had been murdered at that very fort.

I hadn't been the one to discover his body. I hadn't even seen him until the funeral. The only way I had known about the strange circumstances around his death and the markings on his neck was because I had heard the facts from others. And the only reason his killer had ultimately been brought to justice was, again, through the efforts of others, like my amateur detective friend Hannah Hooper. I had been able to do nothing for Jacob, a helplessness I hoped never to experience again.

I took another deep breath, and did my best to push the images from my mind. I couldn't just sit there on the side of the road until it got dark out. I had to keep driving while I still had an hour or so of sunlight left, even if the trees on either side of the road were doing a good job of obscuring all but the brightest beams.

I willed myself to open my eyes, and peered between my fingers at my surroundings.

The Colorado wilderness was vaster than I would have expected. The trees were dense and stretched so far above me that I could barely make out the tops of them. I could only see the sky above the road, where there was a break in the tree line. The clouds were tinged in cotton candy pinks and blues, and they were moving slowly westward toward the sun.

I rubbed my hands over my heavy-lidded eyes, wondering if I'd strapped tiny weights to them. I tried to stifle a yawn, but my eyes were filling with exhausted tears anyways.

"I can't keep going like this..." I muttered to myself, rifling around inside my glove box for a tissue to wipe my eyes with. I wasn't sure if the tears were left over from my nightmare or were just a symptom of the exhaustion.

I grabbed my phone from my purse that was wedged

between a lamp and a box full of mugs and plates, and checked the GPS for the third time that hour. I could really do with some coffee. Strong coffee. Enough to keep an elephant awake would have been just about perfect.

I was still following the right directions to Faerywood Falls, which was the name of the town I was heading toward. I just had to follow this winding road. The road that had been nothing more than trees and tarmac for the last three hours. I couldn't remember the last gas station I'd passed, let alone seeing a hotel since the one I'd stayed at the night before.

It wasn't the worst drive I'd ever taken in my life, but the roads were unfamiliar, and I'd taken a wrong turn more than once, hoping my GPS would just correct itself. Instead, all I did was drain my phone battery and tack on an extra two hours to my already excruciatingly long trip.

I sighed. My ETA was still a long time off, and I had nothing more than a few chocolate bars and some melted ice cubes in the bottom of my water bottle to keep me sated until I got to my destination.

I glanced over my shoulder at the overstuffed vehicle. When I'd purchased this SUV a few years back, I'd never imagined that I'd be using it to pack up all of my belongings and move across the country.

That was a sobering thought. It was like I'd swallowed a heavy weight, staring at boxes full of my books, my clothes, my most precious belongings.

I turned away, gazing back out the windshield. I was crazy, wasn't I?

Yes, I definitely was crazy, but that didn't mean I was doing the wrong thing. I was leaving my old life, taking only the parts worth keeping with me. I was even abandoning my stiff, formal ways in hopes of becoming a warmer person. I had left the practical Prudence behind and would carry the softer name of Marianne from now on. I wondered what Jacob would have thought of that goal.

I let out a heavy exhale before putting the car back into drive, and slowly pulling out onto the completely vacant road. The vehicle that I'd almost run into was the first car I'd seen in almost an hour.

The shadows between the trees were eerie, and so I drove slowly. More than one deer had bolted out in front of me during this epic trek, and I wasn't eager to have my fender completely smashed before I even reached my new home.

Just as the last rays of red light sank beneath the backdrop of the forest, disappearing from sight, I drove past a sign letting me know that I was in Foxglove county. From what I'd read about Faerywood Falls, it seemed as if I was finally, *finally*, in the right place.

"I'm home..." I muttered.

A chill ran down my spine as I heard myself say those words. I stared around, and with a strange sensation, it was as if, for just a moment, I recognized where I was.

I blinked hard a few times, shaking my head.

"It was just de ja vu, nothing more than that," I told myself. "I'm tired, and hungry, and my butt is going to stay permanently numb if I don't stop and get out sooner or later."

Even still, as I continued to drive along, following my GPS closely, I realized that I was relieved. It made sense, obviously. I'd been traveling for two days straight, of course I was relieved.

Suddenly, a flickering movement caused me to gasp again, and I slammed on my brakes.

Two or three dozen shapes burst out of the forest, across

the street, and climbed up into the sky above, their tiny flap-
ping wings only a shade darker than the night that was
falling around me.

Bats. They looked like bats.

But there was nothing scary about bats. This was the
time of night that they came out. I'd seen bats tons of times
growing up in Hillbilly Hollow. Bats were good creatures.
They ate bugs. And didn't bite people. Bats were good.

"I really need to get a grip," I said, taking another deep
breath before easing my foot down on the gas, following the
road in the direction that the bats had taken.

2

I t was just my luck that in addition to the complete darkness that pressed in on my car from all sides, it started to rain big, fat drops. They splattered against my windshield, so loud that it was as if I was being pelted with rocks or ice. For a few seconds, I wondered if it was actually the end of the world, and I was about to get crushed underneath the weight of some falling mountain or something.

I hunched over my steering wheel, my nose nearly pressed against it as I stared out at the road, my two lonely headlights revealing just far enough ahead of me that I had barely enough time to see the abrupt turns and dips that the road was taking me on.

The GPS told me I was less than an hour away. As exhausted as I had been before, I was wide awake now, adrenaline pumping through me like I'd been hooked up to a caffeine I.V. This was the only way to drive. Fear was the very best stimulant.

Lights appeared as I took a sharp corner around a rather ominous looking tree that had branches spanning the whole road, and I saw a sign for a gas station glimmering in the darkness.

My heart leapt. I'd finally found someplace to stop. The gas gage had been making me nervous, and I knew all too well that not only did I not have any food to cook at my new place, I wouldn't have the energy to prepare much anyway.

Microwave something or other it was going to have to be. And in that moment, I really couldn't care at all.

I pulled into the station, which only had one gas pump. A solitary car was parked along the side of the small, brick building.

Hopping out into the chilly night air, I locked my car and headed to the brightly lit front door, some of the creeping fear washing away with the length of the shadows behind me. Cold, fat droplets pelted me as I hurried through the puddles, soaking my shoes all the way through.

A bell sounded when I stepped inside. It smelled of pine cleaning products and freshly grilled hotdogs. The rows were filled with vibrantly colored labels on all sorts of different kinds of candy, snacks and drinks.

"Be with you in one moment," came a woman's voice from the open door behind the long counter at the back.

"Okay," I said back automatically. "I'm just going to use the restroom before I pay for my gas."

"Sounds just fine, dear," the voice replied.

I pulled my jacket a little more tightly around myself before heading between the aisles, my stomach rumbling at the sight of all the junk food.

The restrooms were at the far side of the gas station. These sorts of stops always made me anxious. I feared that touching anything inside those disgusting places was enough to make me contract something awful. But as I stepped into the ladies room, I was pleasantly surprised at how clean it was. The porcelain sink gleamed, the chrome faucet so shiny and polished that I could see my reflection clearly in it. The floor was covered in tiles, and the grout was immaculate, completely mold free.

I even saw a little mason jar filled with fresh flowers sitting on the top of the toilet's tank.

At the sink, I splashed water over my face, the images still stark in my mind from the nightmare. I tried to clear my thoughts completely of whatever was still hanging on in there.

The water was icy cold as it ran from the tap, and it felt rejuvenating just to hold my hands beneath its flow. Mesmerizing, almost. I let some pool in my palms before splashing it onto my cheeks. The shock of the cold stirred me, sending shivers down my spine as I blinked the water from my eyelashes. It felt good.

I didn't even spare myself a glance in the mirror as I grabbed some paper towels to dry my face. I knew that I looked awful, that my eyes were bloodshot, that my skin and hair were greasy, and that my skin was flushed. I needed sleep and a hot shower before I gave my appearance any thought.

It was time to get food. And caffeine. I needed something to survive off of when I finally got to where I was staying.

Leaving the restroom, I walked along until I found the long line of refrigerated drinks and foods. There was every kind of soda I could ever want, along with juice, energy drinks, and bottled water. I grabbed some water and a half a gallon of milk, wondering if there was any cereal here that I could pick up. The idea of something familiar and comforting like that seemed ideal in the moment.

I also managed to grab one of those highly concentrated energy drinks, not really caring if it would keep me up for the next three days. I wasn't so sure I wouldn't just curl up there right on the floor of the gas station and fall asleep.

I managed to find a few frozen dinners. They weren't anything special, but it would get me through a day or two until I could find the nearest grocery store. I worried that if a gas station was this difficult to find, how much harder would other basic human necessities be to come by?

That was just my exhaustion talking, I knew. If people lived all the way out here, then there were definitely things that helped them to survive, including places to buy food.

My hands and arms laden with goodies, I waddled up toward the counter, careful not to tip any of my purchases over the counter and onto the floor.

"There we are," said the woman's voice again. She'd appeared in the doorway.

She was an older lady, with wildly curly red hair. A streak of grey was mingled in there, which she tucked behind her round ear as she smiled at me. She was a plump woman, with rosy cheeks and kind, blue eyes.

Perched on her shoulder was something brown and furry, tinged with grey. It took me a long, hard second to realize that it was a squirrel. A living one, too.

The woman with the squirrel on her shoulder beamed at me across the counter. "Well, good evening, dear. What brings you all the way out here on such a rainy night?"

I stared at her, trying very hard not to look to her left where the squirrel was perched. Out of the corner of my eye, I saw his bushy tail twitch as he nibbled on a large walnut clasped in his tiny paws.

"I needed some gas," I said, pulling my wallet out of my back pocket. "Do you know how far I might be from Faerywood Falls?" I asked. I knew it might be a bit of a reach, but I was getting so tired of driving...

"Sure do, dear," said the woman, picking up my first bag of puffed cheese curls and scanning them before putting them into a plastic bag. "You're about thirty minutes outside of the town limits. If you keep following the road north here, you'll be there in no time."

My hopes jumped. "Really? That close?"

The woman nodded, and the squirrel on her shoulder chittered happily.

There was a rustle behind the counter as the woman picked up my half gallon of milk. I glanced behind the chair that the woman had set up for herself, and saw a raccoon. A rather rotund creature, he seemed intent on crawling into a shallow cardboard box that had been lined with a fleece blanket and pillow. It looked like the perfect nest for a cat, and yet, there went the raccoon.

"My, don't you just have the prettiest shade of hair?" the woman asked, apparently completely unaware or completely okay with the raccoon curling up in the box. "It's like the color of a chestnut. Or earthy, ancient tree bark. It's lovely, dear."

I reached up and twisted my finger around a strand of my hair, all of which had been tied behind my head in a loose ponytail. "Oh...well, thank you," I said. It was something new I was trying lately, wearing my hair loose or in ponytails, instead of pinned up in a formal looking bun all the time, the way it used to be. I'd been told the new look softened me.

"So, what brings you all the way out here to Faerywood Falls?" the woman asked brightly, her smile growing wider as she finished packing up my frozen meals. "You must be new to the area. That's no surprise, really. Visitors come through here all the time on vacation. It's a nice change of pace from all that city life."

"Oh, well, I'm actually just moving into the area," I said, watching my total change on the digital screen above the cash register. It was good to see some modern technology all the way out here in a place that felt like the middle of nowhere.

"Are you really?" the woman asked, almost swelling with excitement. "Well, isn't that just wonderful? It's always so nice to find out that our little town is growing, especially with young people like yourself." She chuckled. "Allow me to be the very first to welcome you here to our humble little town. I hope you'll find it everything you're hoping it is, and that you'll be able to settle right in and call this place home."

The squirrel was attempting to bury itself underneath all that bushy hair of hers, and all I could do was smile in response to her kindness.

"Your total is…oh, heavens, I can't ask you to pay for this, not when you are just moving here! Have the whole lot on me, dear," the woman said, beaming.

"Oh, I couldn't possibly ask you to – " I said.

"*Nonsense*," the woman said. "Please take it as a welcome gift. I know how stressful it can be to move. The last thing you need is something else to be worrying about."

"That's very kind of you," I said.

"And one more thing," she said, holding a finger up and turning around. She knelt down, and just when I was sure I'd hear her shriek in fright at the sight of that raccoon, she surprised me by pushing the box slightly to the side and pulling out a colorful brochure from a stack tucked away in another box. "Here we are," she said, standing back upright. "This is one of those tourist maps that are available at all of the popular destinations around town. There's the old train station restaurant, the antique shops down Main street, and the overlook where you can see the Blackburn castle." She held out the folded map to me, a broad smile on her face. "This should help you get your bearings at first. It shows you the lake, the main lodge for tourists, and the various paths through the forest all through here."

I smiled, reaching out to take the map from her. As my fingers grazed the tips of hers, there was a quick, sharp pulse that sent a shiver up the length of my arm and down my spine. My head throbbed once, and it caused me to withdraw my hand quickly, the map clutched tightly within it.

"I'm sure that'll help you just fine," the woman said, clearly unaware of the shiver I'd felt. She'd already turned to my bags and was hoisting them across the counter toward me. "You'll be very pleased to see that the weather is expected to be much nicer tomorrow."

"Right..." I said, grabbing the bags. "Well, thank you very much."

"Come back and visit sometime soon," the woman said with a wave of her hand, grinning. "I want to know how you're enjoying life in Faerywood Falls!"

"Will do," I said, moving across to the door and shrugging it open with my shoulder, trying hard not to upend any of the bags I was carrying.

I hurried back to the car, tossed the bags inside the backseat wherever I could find room among the boxes, and quickly jumped into the driver's seat.

I sighed, wiping some of the rain from my eyebrows and lashes.

What had that pulse been? It was like I'd been dunked in icy water the way the goosebumps had run up and down my body. Even at the thought, another shiver ran down my back.

I shook my head, and headed back toward the road. A woman with a squirrel and a raccoon for pets. I'd heard of weirder things, but I wasn't ready to write it off as a manifestation of my exhaustion just yet.

I drove on, desperate to find the town.

Not much further now. And then I'd be home.

3

Why my GPS was now telling me that my final destination was almost seven hours away made absolutely no sense to me. It didn't matter what I did. I closed the app, I put in different directions before reentering the address for Faerywood Falls. I'd even shut off my phone, but it didn't matter.

I was glad I'd run into that strange woman at the gas station. She had been very nice, even if just a little weird in her choice of pets. The more I drove, though, the more I became convinced that in my exhaustion, I'd just made the whole thing up. No person in their right mind would let a squirrel hang out on their shoulder like she was. And the raccoon? It must have actually been a cat, or maybe a weird kind of dog. There was no way it was really a raccoon.

I came up over the crest of a hill, and I nearly burst into tears with relief. In the distance, I could see some streetlights. There weren't all that many, but they were the first I'd seen since it got dark, and I was so incredibly ready to be done driving.

The rain had slowed to a gentle pitter patter against my

windshield, which made it easier to see at least a little further on the road. I wasn't all that excited about just how far away those lights were, but the prospect of finally being done with this journey was overwhelming, and all of my anxieties were shoved away.

I drove across a bridge that revealed a gorgeous night sky. I caught a glimpse of lightning darting back and forth between the rain clouds overhead, and found myself excited about seeing what this place looked like in the daylight.

Soon I was surrounded by the trees once more, like thick walls on either side of the road.

My headlights revealed something copper colored in the middle of the road a short ways ahead. I squinted through the rain, trying hard to figure out what it might be. Was it a pipe of some sort that had fallen off the back of a truck? Was it a road cone?

My heart sank as I drew closer. It wasn't any of those things. It was a fox lying on its side.

I slowed the car to a stop, not seeing any cars coming in either direction. I stared out at the little creature.

Poor thing...how terrible it was that someone had hit it and just drove off like that.

There was a lump in my throat as I watched the tiny creature. It had a gorgeous coat, a vibrant orange, with a white belly, black paws, and a tiny black nose.

I was choked up, watching this small, beautiful creature, its tail wrapped around itself as if in an attempt to ward off the inevitable.

Its tail twitched.

My heart jumped.

It was still alive?

Without even thinking, without wasting a second, I jumped out of the car and hurried to the trunk. I threw it open, the rain still coming down, peppering my jacket and hair as I searched with growing frustration for the one thing I knew was in there but couldn't find.

I pulled and pushed boxes out of the way until I found my roadside emergency kit. I tugged the zipper open and rummaged through the flares, the rope, and the jumper cables until I found what I was looking for.

Gloves.

I tugged them on after closing the trunk and hurried toward the fox, who was still bathed in the glow of my headlights.

I cautiously approached, trying not to splash in the puddles all that much. Everything was dark, and all I could hear was the rain.

I bent over the tiny creature, my heart aching as I did. I expected to find a wound, but didn't see anything aside from mud marring the fox's otherwise glorious fur coat. I walked around to stand behind it, letting more of the light wash over the animal.

Then I made a discovery. One of the fox's legs was stretched out behind it, while the others were not. It didn't look broken, but the fox definitely seemed to be nursing it. This close, I could see the rapid rise and fall of its tiny chest.

"It's okay…" I heard myself say in a soothing, quiet tone. "You don't have to be afraid. I'm going to do what I can to help you."

What in the world was I going to do? The only thing that I'd really ever known how to do was accounting, which was the job I'd left to come all the way out here. On weekends, I'd also been a church organist, but that wasn't of any practical help with this situation. I had zero experience with anything to do with animals.

I glanced toward the woods, wondering if I were to carry

the fox over in that direction, if it would just rest until it gained enough strength to run back into the forest. I knew that wouldn't work, though. If it had been strong enough to do that, it probably would have already. And the longer it lay there on the ground, the more likely it became that something bigger and hungry would come along and see the fox as easy prey.

I took a deep breath of the air, heavy with the scent of the rain and wet earth, and knelt down beside the fox.

I reached out with one gloved hand, and gently touched the poor creature on its back.

The fox's black eyes snapped open and it fixed its gaze on me.

Help...

My heart constricted as I stared down into the fox's face. The eyes were alert, and there was an extraordinary depth behind them. Life, and longing. Fear and hope. I could see it all as I stared down into that fox's face.

It was as if I had heard the fox call out for my help... inside my head. But that wasn't possible. The animal was just so frightened, and it was so clear on its dirty face that it needed help, that my tired mind had set my imagination into overdrive, making me think I'd heard some sort of telepathic cry for rescue.

A soft whimper escaped the fox, and I bit down on the inside of my lip.

I couldn't waste any more time. I had to do something to help this fox.

But what?

The fox whimpered again, and I looked up into the surrounding trees. Was there something nearby that only the fox could hear?

I noticed something glowing just inside the tree line. My

headlights reached just the edge of the forest, and beyond that, there was a pair of yellow eyes, staring out at the fox and me in the street.

I swallowed hard. Those eyes were not kind like the fox's. They were sinister, and the sheer size of them made me want to never find out the size of the body they belonged to.

The fox may have sharp teeth and may not exactly like it when I picked it up, but that would be preferable to whatever it was that was staring out at us, perhaps contemplating making the both of us into a meal.

I knew I should have looked up more about this area before moving here. What sort of large creature could be out in those woods?

Without wasting another second, I scooped the fox up into my arms and headed back toward the car. I didn't turn my back on those golden eyes in the forest, though. Whatever it was could have probably made it to us in one leap.

The fox squirmed in my arms, but didn't make any attempts to bite me. Little grunts escaped its muzzle, and I worried that I was hurting its already injured leg.

I opened one of the back doors of the car, trying as hard as I could not to jostle the fox around too much. I kept glancing at the forest. The eyes were still there, watching, waiting.

I upended a box of clothes into the front seat with one hand before grabbing one of my towels that I'd wrapped around a vase to keep it from breaking, and tucking it into the box. As carefully as I would a newborn child, I laid the fox down on the towel.

The fox turned its head to look at me, and my heart squeezed painfully. Was that a look of affection? Worry? Maybe a little bit of both?

Whatever it was, this fox and I had been through something together tonight, and I was going to do my part to help the animal out.

I nestled the fox's box up in the front seat, tucking some of the now loose clothes around it to prevent it from moving around as I drove, and before long was able to hop back into the driver's seat and close the door.

I breathed a sigh of relief, staring out into the darkness.

The golden eyes had disappeared, likely searching for more accessible prey in the depths of the forest.

I puffed out my cheeks, expelling all of the air in my lungs.

"That was close, huh, little buddy?" I asked, putting the car into drive. I pulled off the gloves and set them down beside the fox's box, and peered inside. "You doing okay down there?"

The fox's tail twitched as it stared up at me. I was pleased to see that it was sitting up a little more. For the first time, I feared that it might leap out of the box and try to attack me while I was driving.

Maybe I hadn't thought this all the way through...

I glanced down at my phone, seeing that the GPS app had crashed, and it wouldn't open up again.

I sighed, realizing I was just going to have to keep driving and hope for the best. The lights I'd seen in the distance. That had to be my destination.

Then I could have a hot shower, eat something for the first time all day, and sleep.

Oh, blessed sleep...

"Don't worry, new friend," I said as we started off down the rainy road once again. "I'll call a vet in the area. Or maybe there's a wildlife department or something. There's definitely someone out there who will be able to help you."

At least I hoped there was. Well, I guessed there was always the internet, and maybe someone from a nearby city, nearby being relative, would be able to come out and get the fox.

I glanced into the box again, and saw the fox had settled down as if to sleep, its head on one of its front paws.

The little animal was definitely cute, with its long snout, slender legs, and fluffy orange and white tail.

I shook my head. First a lady with a squirrel and raccoon, and then a fox begging me for help.

There was no way this place could possibly get any weirder.

4

The GPS started working again as soon as I crossed into the Faerywood Falls town limits. There weren't all that many streetlights, but there were some, and the cabin where I was going to be staying wasn't all that far away.

The ride with the fox had been mostly uneventful, the worst thing being the smell of wet animal that filled the car. I realized I probably didn't smell much better, but I also knew that smell would seep into the fabric of the seats and linger for months now.

I sighed.

I took a turn off the main road, which was nothing more than a narrow two lane street, and pulled off onto a dirt lane that divided the forest. I bumped along for a while, trying to avoid potholes, grateful that I was in my SUV and not my mother's tiny hatchback, before breaking through the trees and discovering what must have been the lake.

It was nearly impossible to see. The rain had since cleared, and the moon was trying to peek through some of the clouds. It reflected on the water, but I couldn't for the life of me see the edge of the bank.

I stayed on the road, following it around the lake, passing a few cabins as I did.

This was a place that my mother's sister had picked out for me. I had yet to see it. I hadn't even gotten pictures. Mom said that my aunt claimed it was just fine, and that should be good enough.

Apparently that wasn't all that my aunt, whom I had never met, had arranged for me. Out of the kindness of her heart, she'd also lined up a potential job for me in town.

I was grateful for it. I really was. Especially since she didn't even know me.

The cabin, I soon discovered, was probably nothing to get all too excited about. As I pulled up in front of it, seeing the number *four* in faded white paint on one of the posts on the porch, I was immediately reminded of a cabin that I'd stayed in as a kid when I'd gone to summer camp. This one couldn't have been much bigger.

"Well...Mom said it would be rustic," I said, staring out at the tiny cottage, frowning. "Rustic is right. I wonder if I'll have to sleep on the floor."

I hopped out of the car, and was greeted by the noise of chirping crickets and gurgling bullfrogs. It was a peaceful sound, and it quickly put me at ease. I noticed there was a cute little tree house built into a thick tree in front of the cabin, a feature that would doubtless have been more appreciated by guests with children to enjoy it. Still, it looked fun and whimsical. Maybe this place had some charm to it after all.

"All right, you, let's get you inside before you take off into the night," I said, hefting the box with the sleeping fox out

of the front seat. As carefully as I could, I walked up the
creaking steps to the door.

Right...the key.

I set the box down beside the door and wandered back
down into the yard. A small, thin pine tree that stood on the
front lawn had a low hanging branch, and I spotted the blue
birdhouse swinging from it. Reaching up inside, my fingers
scraped against the cool metal of a key.

Well, at least it was right where I'd been told it would be.

I returned to the porch, picked up my new fox friend,
and unlocked the door.

I stepped over the threshold, and my heart sank as I
switched on the light.

It was small. Very small. As in there were only two
rooms in the entire place, and one of them was a bathroom.

A narrow bed that was covered in patchy quilts stood in
one corner. A kitchenette ran along the wall to my left just
as I entered, and I noticed a small, wooden table beneath a
window that looked barely big enough for one person to sit
at. At least there was a refrigerator. There was also a ratty
couch that was covered in a mustard yellow and pea green
fabric that looked straight out of the seventies, and a wood
stove in the corner that looked as if it hadn't been used in
years.

"I left home...for this?" I asked, closing the door
behind me.

I coughed as I inhaled. A thick layer of dust and musti-
ness had settled in over the whole cabin. I wasted no time
turning to one of the windows and shoving it open. It stuck
a little, and I made a mental note to try and fix it later. If I
was going to have to live in such a tiny place, I was going to
need to make the most of it.

I walked the short distance from the door to the couch,

where I gently set the box with the sleeping fox down. I debated about putting it in the bathroom but I wanted first dibs so I could shower.

I turned around and stared out the window at the car, still completely packed with all of my stuff, including a toothbrush, pajamas, and all the food I'd gotten at the gas station.

With a groan, I trudged back out into the night to get the minimal amount of items I'd need to make it until morning.

LATER, as I let my hair air dry and my food heat up in the tiniest and loudest microwave I had ever seen, I used the internet on my phone to search for a local wildlife service. It was after midnight, and I knew it was a long shot, but I tried to call them anyway.

There was no answer and no way to leave a message, so I hung up and tried to find a veterinarian in the area. I was glad to see that there was one...and only one. I sighed, dialing the number. It was no surprise when he didn't answer. I left a message on his machine.

"Hi, my name is Marianne Huffler, and I just moved into the area. While I was out driving tonight, I happened to find an injured fox on the side of the road. I brought it home with me, worried that it might get killed. It's sleeping right now. I think it's okay? Anyway, please call me back. My number is..." After leaving my number with the machine, I sighed and hung up. It wasn't like I had actually expected anyone to answer, especially not this late. Even still, it would have been nice to have some help.

I got up from the arm of the chair where I was sitting, and walked over to the box, peering inside. The fox had curled up in a tight ball, and I watched the even rise and fall of its chest. It was sleeping, and pretty soundly, too.

I ate as much of the microwave noodles as I could before I just couldn't keep my eyes open any longer. I dragged myself over to the bed, snatching my pillow off the floor along the way, and collapsed onto the mattress. I didn't even care that the blankets weren't mine. At that point, I knew that I could probably sleep on a cold rock.

I rolled over onto my side and realized I could see the night sky out the window. The stars were so clear out there. It was like the entire sky was made of them.

It reminded me of the night that my mother had told me...well, everything.

"Prudence? Dear, there is...something that I need to tell you. I need you to sit down to hear this, all right?" Mom had said.

"You're acting like someone's died, Mom," I'd said. *"What's going on?"*

She'd sighed, her eyes puffy. *"After this whole thing that happened with Peter Snipes, I've realized I have to tell you the truth."*

"The truth? The truth about what?" I asked.

She gave me a hard look in that moment. *"All of these terrible tragedies that have happened to you and around you, especially this most recent one that nearly cost you your life... haven't they ever seemed strange to you?"*

"Of course they have," I had said. *"First Jacob was murdered, and then after I'd managed to meet Peter, another man who I could love, a man who eventually asked me to marry him, he turned on me and tried to kill me."*

My mom had gone pale, like the beautiful moonlight streaming in through the windows of her kitchen, as we had sat around the table. It had always been just her and me in that tiny cottage on the outskirts of Hillbilly Hollow,

Missouri. Even after I had grown older and moved into a place of my own, I had still spent a lot of my time over at my mom's. We Huffler women mostly kept to ourselves and liked our quiet life.

"What if I told you there was a way to break your cycle of bad luck?" she asked in such a low voice that I had almost missed her words entirely.

"I wouldn't call it a cycle," I said.

"You're right, that's not the right word for it..." she said, as serious as I'd ever seen her. *"It's a curse. And there is only one way to break it."*

She then proceeded to turn my entire world upside down by telling me that I was not, in fact, her daughter. Not by blood, anyway. She'd adopted me when I was only an infant. She'd found me in a basket in a forest when she was visiting her sister in the Colorado mountains one summer. She also told me there had been a note tucked into my basket. The note said that the child must remain in Faerywood Forest, and if she did not, then she would be cursed, plagued with misfortune until she returned to that spot.

Misfortune didn't even scratch the surface.

"I didn't believe it at the time but now I do, and I see there is only one answer," my mother had said. *"You have to return to the place of your birth. It's the only way to break your curse."*

A curse, huh? Even though it had been several weeks since that conversation, I wasn't any closer to believing in curses. Sure, I'd had bad luck in the romance department. I'd fallen head over heels for "Preacher Jacob", the pastor at the little church in Hillbilly Hollow, but he hadn't returned my affections. He wound up dead not all that long after I'd confessed my feelings for him.

That heartbreak ended up introducing me to Peter Snipes, the funeral director at the home where Jacob's services were held. Peter had been so kind to me, noticing how much I was hurting even though I wasn't Jacob's family. We started spending a lot of time together, and one date led to another, and before I knew it, he'd proposed.

I had never been so happy.

At least, I was happy until I discovered a terrible secret about the crooked way Peter ran his business, a secret that made him feel so threatened that he had poisoned me to keep me silent.

The next time I opened my eyes, I was hooked up to tubes and wires, with the sterile lights of a hospital shining down on me. I'd been told he'd tried to kill me and nearly succeeded.

The idea of restarting my life, away from all of that pain and heartache was definitely appealing. Whispers followed me wherever I went around town, and I was tired of all the pitying stares. Even if I didn't stay here in Faerywood Falls, Colorado, permanently, it would still give me a chance to let the dust settle and allow people back home to move on with their lives.

The idea of leaving my mother was a lot harder, but finding out that I was adopted so long ago was something that was going to take me some time to come to grips with anyway. And what better place for that than the spot where I was supposedly born?

My mother never found that note again, the one she'd discovered tucked into the basket with me when she'd stumbled upon my crying form in the middle of the Colorado woods. The note had been lost over the years since. But I didn't need to see the message to believe the story, strange as it was. My mom had never lied to me.

Anyway, all of that was in the past now. I had put my sad

story behind me and was ready to move on with a new life in a new place, with any luck.

Gazing out the window at the starry sky over Faerywood Falls, I hoped that the morning would bring goodness with it. The image of the bats fluttering over the road and the golden eyes staring at me from the depths of the trees sent a fresh shiver down my spine as I closed my eyes.

I didn't want to tempt fate, but...

What could go wrong next?

5

I t was as if I'd just drifted off to sleep. My dreams were filled with dancing lights and lapping water against a shore. The moon hung high above, and every once in a while, I could have sworn that I heard it sing.

Bang bang bang.

I sat straight up, my heart pounding in my chest.

It was morning. Bright, warm light streaked in through the windows. In the glow of the new day the panes looked as if they hadn't been cleaned in years. There was a rich smell of cedar as the sunshine washed over the wood of the small cabin. A layer of dew clung to the branches outside the windows.

Bang bang bang.

I blinked, looking around. What was making that racket?

My foggy mind suddenly seemed to switch on, and the memories of the night before came flooding back to me. The gas station. The golden eyes. The fox.

The fox.

I leapt out of bed and hurried over to the box, peering inside.

The animal was gone.

Where could it be? I whirled around and looked all over the floors, the couch, and glanced under the bed. The fox was nowhere to be seen.

The only evidence of it that I found was the torn package of food from my dinner the night before. Apparently, my furry visitor had helped itself to my leftovers after I'd fallen asleep.

With a groan, I turned and figured out where it had gone. The window I'd opened last night was still cracked, and there was definitely a big enough gap for a fox to slip through.

A woman's face suddenly appeared behind the glass, and I jumped.

She was shorter than I was, with white hair and piercing blue eyes. Her face was round with a small chin and a narrow, pointed nose that somewhat reminded me of a bird's beak.

She was wearing what looked like a beekeeper's hat without the netting, and a shirt that belonged on a safari, not in the middle of the forest.

"Good to see you're up and about already," the woman said with a firm nod and a smile. "It's best to make sure that the early bird catches the worm, right? Good for you."

I glanced down at myself and wondered what she meant. I was still in my pajamas, and the room inside looked like a mess, even though I hadn't brought all that much in with me the night before. Did it look like I was busy working instead of snoozing the morning away?

"Uh...thanks," I said, not really sure what to say. "I don't mean to be rude, but...who are you?"

The woman tipped her hat. "The name's Mrs. Bickford,

the owner of this little slice of heaven that you're renting. Which makes me your new landlady."

"Oh, well it's very nice to meet you," I said, reaching for my jacket on the back of one of the chairs. "If you give me just a second to change, I'll come out and greet you properly."

"That'd be good. There are a few things I wanted to go over with you," she said. She turned her head and looked up, her brow suddenly furrowing as she put her hands on her hips. "No, Jim, I won't forget."

"Sorry?" I asked.

She looked back at me. "Oh, nothing, dear. It's just my husband. He's always nagging me about this or that. You'll learn how it goes when you get married."

I couldn't see anyone standing out there with her, but that didn't mean he wasn't just off to the side, or maybe down off the porch.

I quickly grabbed my overnight bag from beside the bed and ran into the bathroom. I hastily changed into something that would be more suitable for moving all of my stuff inside, brushed my teeth, and rushed back outside.

Mrs. Bickford was standing on the porch overlooking the lake that I could now fully see in the light of day.

It was magnificent. The lake was wide and long. I could see the other side, where other tiny cabins were dotted around the shore. The same dense, thick forest pushed right up to the edge of the water, the dark green pines and spruces all stretching upward toward the beautiful, cloudless sky.

The water rippled as a gentle breeze passed over its surface, and it reached the two of us standing there on the porch, ruffling my hair ever so slightly. It carried the earthy scent of the grass and the musky smell of fresh water lakes.

The view alone eased my anxious heart, and helped me to relax a little.

"So, Prudence, isn't it?" Mrs. Bickford asked, turning to me.

"Actually, I'm going by Marianne now," I said.

She didn't question that, just nodded up at me, a look of determination on her face. "Well, I'm glad to see that you found the key to the cabin, Marianne. How was your first night?"

"Great," I said. "I was so ready to sleep when I finally got here."

"What time was that? After midnight?" the woman asked. "I saw your headlights pull in."

I said, "Oh, I'm really sorry if I woke you up or anything. I didn't mean to be so loud."

"You were fine," Mrs. Bickford said. "Now, there were a couple of things I wanted to show you." She turned and stepped right into the cabin, leaving the door open for me to follow after.

I blinked and followed her inside.

"Now, this place may be small, but I like to think the tight size just makes the cabins cozy. Besides, I heard you're looking to move into the area permanently from Missouri," she said, walking over to the fridge and pulling the door open. "Should be a nice place to get your feet off the ground."

"Yeah," I agreed, a twinge of nervousness flooding through me. "How did you know that?"

"Your aunt told me," she said, pulling a water bottle out of the fridge. "Would you like one, too?"

"Sure," I said, wondering why the woman was going through my fridge and asking if I wanted anything. "So do you know my aunt well, then?"

"Very well, yes," she said. "My husband and I have been friends with your family for many, many years. She's a special lady, your aunt. And so is that cousin of yours. She really knows her way around a – well, lookie here. I see that Mr. Gibbs did get here yesterday to fix that ice maker. Good to see, good to see." She turned to me and planted her hands on her hips again. "Now, if you ever need anything, and if something breaks, or you spring a leak or anything like that, you just let me know, and I'll let Mr. Gibbs know, and he'll come right over. He's a real hoot, that one. He likes to talk about the *old days*. Where everything around Faerywood Falls was as it was meant to be."

"And how is that?" I asked as I watched her move over to the stove, pull open the door and peer inside.

"Well, quieter for one," she said, running her finger along the wire racks inside. "All these tourists around have made life here a little more...well, difficult, as it were. Those of us who have lived here for generations don't much like the company. It messes with our ability to do – oh, good, I did leave a broom here for you. Silly me, I'd borrowed it a few weeks ago and...oh, dear, this isn't a bed for a pet, is it?"

She'd stopped over the box on the couch where the fox had been sleeping the night before. The look she gave me was like a teacher who'd caught a misbehaving student in the act.

"No, not a pet," I said. "It was – "

"Because you know that you aren't allowed to have pets here," Mrs. Bickford said. "My husband is highly allergic, and we've had too many accidents over the years with people's precious pets getting lost in the forest. I'd had enough of the reports."

"That makes sense to me," I said nervously.

Mrs. Bickford sighed and looked about. "Well, I should

get out of your hair. Jim tells me that I talk too much and make our guests uncomfortable. I just wanted to make sure you knew you were welcome, and be certain that everything was working well enough for you. Oh, that reminds me. The door to the bathroom sticks sometimes. Just twist the handle to the right and it should pop open, okay?"

"Sure, sounds good," I said.

"I left my number on that note on the fridge for you," she said, pointing to the refrigerator door. "Call anytime you need anything, but only call after nine if it's an emergency. Oh, and I'm not home on Thursdays. That's bingo night and Jim hates to miss it."

"Right," I said, nodding. "I will make sure to only call if it's a real emergency."

Mrs. Bickford grinned at me. "And don't be a stranger. We are neighbors now, after all. You ever make an extra pie and need someone to give it away to, don't hesitate to ask." She wiggled her fingers over her shoulder as she marched toward the door, stepping back out into the morning light washing over the lake in ripples. "Tata, Marianne. Have a great first day, and welcome to Faery-wood Falls!"

She promptly closed the door behind her.

Through the window, though, I heard her voice again. "See? I told you I can make myself scarce... No, I don't need you to remind me, thank you, dear."

I stared out after her, not seeing anyone anywhere nearby.

Who was she talking to? It sounded like her husband, but he definitely wasn't there.

Great. My landlady was crazy.

I sank down onto the end of the bed, brushing my hair from my eyes. I'd met more than my fair share of interesting people, but interesting and nosy? Mrs. Bickford was going to require a constant watch, wasn't she?

I stared around at the small space, wondering if even the little I had brought was actually going to fit inside. I'd easily fill the armoire, and the tiny linen closet in the bathroom would hardly be able to hold all my towels and blankets and sheets.

I had to keep reminding myself that this didn't have to be where I lived for the rest of my life. It was for now.

And with that view…I could really get used to seeing that lake all the time.

There was an angry buzzing sound behind me that made me jump. It was my phone, vibrating so hard it was trying to knock itself off the table.

I raced over to it, snatching it out of the air before it could fall, and answered it.

"Hello. Is this Marianne?" asked the voice on the other end.

"Yes, this is her," I said.

"This is Dr. Brian Henson, the veterinarian that you left a message with last night?" the man said. He had a kind voice that was easy to listen to. "So, you found a fox, huh?"

I gave him a quick recap of what had happened – leaving out the part where I could have sworn the fox was asking me for help inside my brain – and he listened patiently the whole way through.

"Well, it sounds like you already know what I'm going to tell you, but it's unsafe to be handling wild animals. They might bite and be carriers of disease. But, I can admire your heroism and desire to help the poor creature. It's probably for the best that the fox recovered enough and took off without injuring you or itself any further."

"Right," I said.

"Foxes are quite common around here, and while they're not likely to harm a human, it's definitely best to keep your distance from them," he said.

"Will do," I said. "Thanks so much for getting back to me."

"Sorry I couldn't have been more help last night," he said. "I would just advise not taking in any more wild strays."

I laughed. "Definitely not."

"Is there anything else?" he asked.

Part of me thought to ask about the eyes I'd seen in the woods, but now that I was feeling much more refreshed, I wasn't sure I hadn't just made that whole thing up in my exhaustion. "Nope. Thanks so much for your time, Dr. Henson."

"Of course. Have a good day."

I glanced over at the open window and frowned.

I wondered where the little fox had gotten to...and if it was all right.

6

I stood there in front of my SUV for nearly five minutes before I realized just how much I didn't want to unpack. My back was still sore from being stuck driving for two days straight, and the sheer number of boxes seemed to multiply every time I peeked my head inside the car.

That, and Mrs. Bickford's mention of my aunt and cousin made me think that it might be better to show them my face sooner rather than later. If Mom called and let them know I was here, they might wonder why I hadn't come to see them yet.

I sighed, grabbing one of the bags of chips that I'd picked up from the gas station the night before, and hopped back into my car. I ignored the fact that I could barely see out the back window, and continued on down the road, following my now functional GPS to the lakeside lodge where I would find my aunt and my cousin.

All of the eeriness seemed to vanish with the night. The forest was beautiful. Birds sang to one another as I drove along the dirt road with my window down. I caught sight of fish jumping in the lake, their splashes causing swells in the otherwise mirror-like surface. The air was warm and the day was bright.

A flicker of something silver caught my eye ahead, and I quickly slammed on my brakes as a dog jumped out in front of me.

My heart hammering against my ribs, I peered out of the windshield at the creature.

My chest tightened. It wasn't a dog at all.

It was a wolf.

It had gleaming silvery grey fur, a long snout, dark nose, and golden eyes. And the wolf was staring straight at me.

I gripped the steering wheel as if it might give me some support. I was fully protected inside the vehicle, yet something about that wolf's gaze unsettled me. It was as if it was watching me with an intelligent gaze, as if it was regarding me as its equal, not as prey or predator.

I swallowed nervously as the wolf turned its shaggy head away, and it started to walk off the road and into the tree line.

I couldn't swallow past the lump in my throat. Those eyes...they reminded me way too much of the eyes I'd seen the night before in the woods. It must have been a wolf that had stared out of the trees at me then. This couldn't be the same wolf, could it? We were miles away from where I'd found the fox...

I pushed the wolf out of my mind, but even still, I took more caution as I drove up the road toward the lodge.

The structure came into view a short while later. It was tucked away up on a hill that overlooked the lake and all the cabins that surrounded it. As my SUV snaked up through the winding roads, I could see the appeal of this place as a tourist destination. It was so lovely here, so peaceful. I could understand why Mom liked coming to visit her sister here.

The lodge itself was a grand sight, with a lot of large windows around to let all that glorious light in. It looked almost as big as some hotels I'd seen, but it felt a lot more homey.

I hopped out of the car and headed toward the front entrance, checking over my shoulder for any other animals that wanted to jump out at me.

Nothing decided to, and that helped me to breathe a little easier.

I stepped inside and was blown away by the luxuriousness of the lodge. I wasn't sure if I expected to see bearskin rugs or antler chandeliers, but instead I found overstuffed leather sofas, hand carved wooden tables, and paintings of the lake that were as long as my new cabin was wide.

"Good afternoon, Miss," came the voice of a man behind a counter off to the side. He had a large white moustache that obscured his mouth, but his eyes told me he was smiling. "Are you checking in?"

"Actually, I'm looking for Candace Brooks," I said. "She's my aunt. I think she's expecting me."

The man nodded and disappeared behind a door.

A moment later, the door opened, and the kind, elderly man was followed by two women who looked very much like...and very much like my mother. Like her, they both had beautiful dark hair. Also like her, they both kept it long. The younger kept it in a long braid that fell down her back, and the elder wore it loose, all full of volume and shine. They both had green eyes, rosy cheeks, and wide hips, just like my mother.

"You must be Prudence," the older of the two women said, stepping out from behind the counter. The only reason

I could tell her apart from her daughter was because of her years and the fact she was a little fuller figured. Otherwise, my aunt and cousin could have been twins. She held out her hand to me, smiling. "I'm your Aunt Candace."

"Nice to meet you," I said, taking her hand and shaking it. I added, "I'm actually going by my middle name of Marianne nowadays."

"I'll try to remember that," she said, smiling. Her grip was gentle, but warm, and there was pure joy in her eyes as she patted the back of my hand with her own. She looked over beside her and gestured to the girl standing next to her, her hair tied back in a braid. "And this is your cousin, Bliss. She's only a year younger than you are."

Bliss smiled at me, and we shook hands as well. I noticed this close that she had a tiny sapphire stud in her left nostril. Her eyes widened as she looked more closely at me. "Wow... you have silver eyes," she said, her mouth hanging open slightly. She looked over at her mother. "Did you see her eyes, Mom?"

Her mother smiled kindly. "Yes, I did. They are very pretty."

Sheepish, I smiled and looked away. My whole life, I'd been complemented on the color of my eyes. I'd always thought they were grey, which I knew was a rare enough color, but this was the first time I'd heard the word *silver* used.

"So, how was your trip up here?" Aunt Candace asked warmly, brushing some of her thick, dark hair behind her ear. "Uneventful, I hope?"

"For the most part, yeah," I said with a smile, reflecting on the woman at the gas station and the fox. "I got in late last night. I don't think I've ever been happier to have a bed to sleep in."

"Are you hungry at all?" Bliss asked. "We just finished breakfast and had some leftovers."

"No thank you, I'm fine. I ate on my way up here," I said. The greasy chips hadn't done much to fill me up, but the nervousness at meeting new people had my stomach twisted in knots enough to kill whatever appetite I did have.

"Well, why don't we show you around?" Aunt Candace said. "I hope that you'll be able to call this place home just like we have."

"That's very kind of you," I said.

Bliss fell into step beside me, a little smirk crawling up the side of her face. Her eyes were so startlingly green that I found it hard to look away. "How do you like the cabin Mom found you?" she asked.

"Oh, it's very nice," I said. "It's cozy, the perfect size for one person."

Bliss laughed and her mother arched an eyebrow at her.

"I know it wasn't much," Aunt Candace said to me. "But it was close to us and something that was more than afford-able. You could have stayed here at the lodge, of course, but I thought you might enjoy the peace and privacy of having your own space."

"I think I will," I said. "That view is spectacular."

"Just wait until you see it from these windows at the top of the stairs," Bliss said as we started to climb a gorgeous staircase carpeted in plush green. "I've heard the Missouri hills are pretty and all, but Colorado has her own kind of charm."

We reached the top of the stairs, and she couldn't have been more right. The lake was spectacular. It looked almost perfectly round from up here, and the landscape looked as if it had been painted on with a thick, bristly brush.

"You must be missing your mom already, aren't you?"

Aunt Candace asked suddenly. I turned and saw her eyes were on me, and she looked a little sad.

"A bit," I admitted. "Though everything she'd told me before I left...it's all kind of hard to believe, you know? It's hard to think that I was adopted."

"But that doesn't mean you are any less a part of our family," Bliss said, throwing an arm around my shoulders and winking at me. "There are some things that are thicker than blood, you know."

Her mother gave her a cautioning look I didn't understand, and Bliss smiled nervously and stepped away.

These women were already treating me like family. They were being so kind, so open with me. I realized how much I was already starting to like them.

"It's a relief having people here who are so normal," I said without thinking. "I feel like my last couple days have just been so weird. It's nice to be reminded that my whole life isn't upside down."

Bliss furrowed her brow. "Weird? What do you mean by weird?"

I shrugged. "Well, my landlady for one. She's...well, she's a character."

"Mrs. Bickford?" Aunt Candace asked.

I nodded.

"She's harmless enough," Bliss said. "She may be way nosier than she needs to be – by the way, she'll remind you if you leave your porch light on all night – but other than that, she wouldn't hurt a fly."

"It wasn't that," I said. I shifted uncomfortably. "She was talking to thin air. She kept saying these things about her husband and then turning to look at nothing and talking like he was asking her questions."

Bliss and Aunt Candace exchanged a very similar look.

"She has a tendency to do that, yes," Aunt Candace said.

"But she's perfectly harmless," Bliss said. "Now, come with me. I want to show you the lodge's pool and hot tub."

My spirits perked up. "Hot tub? Really?" Though I wasn't exactly ready to drop the whole Mrs. Bickford thing, as I had the sneaking suspicion they weren't telling me everything, I was willing to let it go for now and let them show me around.

Aunt Candace grinned at us both. "I just knew the two of you would get along."

They walked with me all over the whole resort. It held tons of rooms, all lavishly furnished. I met a lot of the staff, all of whom were busy cleaning and arranging and cooking and preparing. Apparently we were headed into one of the more popular tourist seasons of the year. Everything was so pretty, and I heard myself promise over and over again that I would come up to visit them here.

As we were nearing lunchtime, we'd found our way to the back of the resort where the pools were. They had an indoor and outdoor pool, as well as a hot tub that was both inside and outside, connected by an opening in the wall. Bliss mentioned that sitting in the hot tub as it snowed was basically magical.

Her mother had given her another look for that comment. Was she not supposed to be in the hot tub when it snowed?

I was wandering through the locker room when I heard Bliss say something to her mother in a hushed tone.

"So...that hunter died?" she asked. "The one who was attacked in the forest last night?"

A chill ran down my spine. A dead hunter? I pretended to examine the list of all the activities offered for guests while I listened to what they were saying.

"Yes," I heard Aunt Candace say heavily. "Unfortunately, he passed away early this morning."

"That's the third one this month," Bliss said.

"I know..." Aunt Candace said solemnly. "It's happened far too often to be coincidence."

"Do you think it could have been him?" Bliss asked.

Her mother made a noise to silence her. "Of course not," she said in a much more motherly whisper. "He would never go that far, or allow any of the others to, either."

"So you really think whatever attacked him was... normal?" Bliss asked.

"Probably only a bear or a wolf," Aunt Candace said. "He was just at the wrong place at the wrong time. Just like all the others."

"Of all the places..." said Bliss. "To be killed by the ordinary kind."

My stomach twisted painfully. So much for this place not being weird.

"Ordinary what?" I asked, walking back over to them.

They both seemed flustered as I approached. "Oh, nothing, dear," Aunt Candace said with a broad grin, even though there were spots of embarrassed color in her cheeks.

"Some hunters have been killed in the woods recently," Bliss said. "The police are baffled."

Aunt Candace stepped between us. "Actually, Marianne, there was something I meant to ask you earlier. Did your mother tell you that I managed to find you a job in town?"

"Yeah, she mentioned it," I said. "What sort of job is it?"

"Oh, you're going to *love* it," Bliss said, nodding fervently.

"It's nothing too strenuous," Aunt Candace said. "Most days, you will probably find yourself reading a lot of the time. Very relaxed."

"That sounds nice," I said. I was still looking back and

forth between them with curiosity. What had they been talking about, *really*?

"If you want, I could take you into town and you could meet the owner, see if this might be something you're interested in," Aunt Candace said.

"What, like, now?" I asked.

She nodded. "I know it's a lot, and you just got here, but he really needs the help, and I really think you'll like working for him."

It was sudden, but what else did I have to do all day? "Okay, that sounds great," I said, flickers of anxiety fluttering inside me like hummingbirds.

"Wonderful," Aunt Candace said. "We shouldn't delay, then. Bliss, you make sure that old Mr. Terrance has his lunch break today, all right? He's not taken one for three days."

"Yes, Mom," Bliss said with a wink at me. "Have fun in town. Say hi to Mr. Cromwell for me."

7

"So tell me, Marianne," Aunt Candace asked as we drove along in her car through the winding roads. "How are you liking Faerywood Falls so far?"

I pulled my gaze away from the river that rushed below the bridge we were crossing, the foamy white waves crashing against the slick, rocky cliffs flanked by more thick forest. "It's absolutely beautiful," I said. "I've never been here, but even still it feels so welcoming."

Aunt Candace smiled. "Some people will always feel that way, returning to the place where they're from. Some would even say that the soil sings to them in a way it would sing for no other." She gave me a gentle smile. "An old wives tale, of course, but I like the sentiment. Makes me feel like we all have a place to belong in this world, you know?"

I understood her perfectly. The trees, so tall and dark, hovered over my head like guardians. I wasn't someone they were trying to keep out. I was being protected. I couldn't explain it, but I was feeling more and more secure as time went on.

"Now, this town is a little humbler than some places, but

I think you'll find that while we don't have thirty choices for bottled water at the grocery store, we more than make up for it in small town charm and quality."

As she spoke, we rounded a corner, and the town came into view. It was tucked away in a shallow valley, with mountains far in the distance beyond. A river ran right through the middle, with small bridges connecting the houses and shops that were dotted around among the trees.

It certainly was humble, but that didn't matter. There was a Mom and Pop shop on the corner right beside the river. According to the store's sign, it sold milk and eggs at rock bottom prices. A grocery store that was not a chain stood open along the main street that only had one stoplight. I saw a gas station in the distance, and there wasn't a mall or a pretentious coffee shop in sight.

"It's like stepping back in time," I said, staring out at a few people walking down the sidewalks, waving to others on the opposite side of the street.

"Your mother told me you have quite an interest in history," Aunt Candace said with a grin. She brushed some of that gorgeous dark hair behind her ears again. "That's what gave me the idea for this job for you."

"I do love history," I said. "I wanted to be a history teacher, but I had a hard time with some of the classes in college. I discovered I was pretty natural at accounting, and went with that, instead."

"I heard you used to be an organist, as well," Aunt Candace said.

My heart twisted uncomfortably. That was something that still brought out the memory of Jacob, as I hadn't played since his death. He'd asked me to come and play at the local church, which I had happily done for a long time, partly because it had given me a chance to be close to him.

"Yeah, I did. The church I attended was this old, 19th century building that I fell in love with. I always wondered what sort of stories a place like that held that we would never know."

Aunt Candace smiled wider. "I really think you're going to love this place, then."

She pulled into a small parking lot of a shop that was situated at the top of a hill, overlooking the valley. A short ways away, further down the road, I could see a diner, and I remembered passing a flea market that was open three days a week.

A tattered, old sign swung in the breeze, revealing the name *Abel's Antiques*.

"An antique shop?" I asked, my heart skipping a beat. "Really?"

She nodded as she hopped out of the car. "Come on, I'll introduce you to old Abe Cromwell."

A tiny bell rang as we stepped in through the front entrance. The ancient door looked like it had come off a castle or something, lined with iron and adorned with a heavy lock.

It smelled of old books and dust inside. Shelves lined every wall, and formed narrow aisles throughout the rest of the shop. It seemed to offer something for everyone: silverware, lamps, sewing machines, and mismatched furniture. I saw a faded globe that had become almost amber it was so discolored, and a pair of golden scales that caught the light just right as it filtered in through the grimy windows. It was beautiful and sad all at the same time. These pieces, once so important to someone at some point in time, had ended up here, forgotten on a shelf.

"Mr. Cromwell?" Aunt Candace called, walking between a shelf of glass mixing bowls and old gelatin molds. "It's

Mrs. Brooks. I brought that nice young lady for you to meet."

The shadows near the back of the room seemed to waver, and a man appeared. It took me a second to realize it was just a pair of black curtains that he'd parted and stepped through.

He was a portly sort of man, with a round belly and thick hands. His head was balding and what little hair he did have was as white as snow. He wore spectacles on the end of his nose, and looked at me over the top of them, his nose wrinkling as he drew closer.

"Candace, good afternoon," he said in a wheezy voice. "I'm glad to see you."

"Nice to see you too, Abe," she said with a smile. "This is Marianne Huffler, my sister's girl. She's come to stay with us out here in Faerywood Falls for awhile."

He looked me up and down. "I hear that you like history, young lady," he said. "That would make you a good fit for this job. See, I'm getting old. I had a terrible illness a few years back, and then a fall a few months ago has really taken the strength out of me. Running this place is such a joy, but I just can't keep up with it anymore. I'm not looking for much, just someone to help me manage the day to day workings so the store can reopen."

I looked over at my aunt, and saw her nod encouragingly at me.

"He lives up in the apartment above the shop, so if you ever needed anything, he said you'd be able to come ask him. And Mr. Cromwell here has some very interesting stories that I'm sure you'd love to hear."

Abe smiled, and I saw one of his lower teeth was actually gold. "Faerywood Falls is a special place. It's where my wife wanted to end up one day. And we did. It's the only place I've ever lived where I've felt such peace and security."

I smiled at him. "I'm starting to see why so many people like this place, myself."

His grin widened. "Well, if your aunt can vouch for you like she has, then you've got the job, my dear. I'm anxious to get this store up and running again."

"The rest of the townsfolk will love to hear that you are reopening," Aunt Candace told him.

He told me my hours and what my pay would be, which was incredibly generous, as well as gave me a key. It was a thick iron key that was as long as my palm. He said there were only two of them, and I now had the second.

"And you're sure you're all right starting on Monday?" asked Abe, looking at me intently over the top of his glasses.

"Of course," I said. I knew that I was going to need money sooner or later. "I really only need a couple of days to unpack."

He nodded. "Well, if you're sure." His eyes suddenly widened. "Oh, Candace, there was something Bliss asked me to set aside for her earlier this year that I had completely forgotten about until you called last week. Would you mind coming with me upstairs to fetch it?"

"Of course," Aunt Candace said.

Abe gestured toward the counter. "You go ahead and get yourself acquainted with things, Marianne. We'll be back in a jiffy."

I watched them walk toward the black curtains separating the rooms.

Tucking the huge key into the pocket of my jacket, I started wandering around, looking at things more closely. The cash register was in the back, and it looked simple enough to use. I found a record keeping book, and noticed there wasn't a computer in sight. I found a glass cabinet that was locked that seemed to house more valuable items, like jewelry and real silver candlesticks. There was a fine layer of dust on nearly everything. It really must have been a while since this place had been open.

My eyes fell on the book section, and I made my way over, perusing the selections that Abe had collected over the years. There were a lot of travel guides for the area that had to have been written in the seventies. There were cookbooks, nature books, and a rather impressive collection of books about fishing. With all the great rivers and lakes around, it didn't surprise me.

I spotted a dusty, faded red tome on the end of the second row, wedged in between the wood and a set of paperback novels. It had golden writing down the spine, but some of the letters had faded and I couldn't make out the title.

Curiosity overtook me as I pulled the book off the shelf. It looked so old, and it was so different than all the others that I just couldn't help myself. I wondered if it belonged in a museum instead of an antiques shop.

When I flipped it open, I wasn't sure what to expect. Maybe some sort of storybook for children, or historical accounts or documents. Instead, I found lines of letters, from the top of the page down to the bottom, all in neat rows. It was as if I was staring at some strange word search.

The letters were all written in a shimmering blue ink that seemed to almost shift and change before my eyes. A letter *C* suddenly became an *S*, and I wasn't sure that I hadn't just made up the whole thing in my mind.

I scratched at my chin, wondering how on earth Abe had come across a book like this. Did he even know he had it? How long had it been sitting there?

I flipped through the pages, and there was nothing

obvious to distinguish one set of pages from the next. No chapter headings, no numbers anywhere.

It was so strange.

The only thing that seemed to change at all was the letters themselves. I assumed it was just the light playing tricks on my eyes, since the ink was so iridescent, but I couldn't be sure.

They were definitely letters I recognized, so whatever it said, it was written in an original Latin language. What was strange, though, was how it was written in an almost Asiatic way, up and down. It made me wonder if it also read from right to left, too.

The blue text glimmered beneath my gaze, and I scrolled my finger down the page.

It doesn't make any sense, I thought. *This whole row here are consonants. You couldn't speak this if you tried.*

"H, D, T, G, K..." I read. *Could it be an acronym for something? But the whole book couldn't be an acronym, could it?*

Suddenly excited, I kept flipping pages, wondering if I'd stumbled upon something encrypted. It was as if I was in a movie, and this was the climax of the whole story.

I paused when the color of the ink suddenly changed. It was now a rosy red, and still glimmered as if written in an ink dusted with the finest of glitter.

And a word had appeared on the page, too. Something that at least looked like a word.

Ressen.

Ressen. What could that mean? Was it a name? Was it a place?

I chewed on the inside of my lip. It was the word that made up the first column on the right side of the page.

"*Ressen...*" I whispered.

It was as if I could taste the word on my tongue. It was

sweet, like honey or maple syrup. It filled my mind, echoing like the gonging of a bell, reverberating around inside of me like light bouncing off a mirror.

The book in my hands suddenly became very light. I stared down at it, wondering why I couldn't feel it against my skin anymore.

I gasped as I saw the book hovering in the air, just above my hands, as if it were caught in an anti-gravity chamber.

I could only stare. There was a dim shimmering light that was emanating from around the pages, bathing my fingertips in a blue glow. A hum filled my ears, but I couldn't find its source. It was soothing, like a salve for my soul.

I was imagining this. My brain had finally snapped. All the stress of the last few weeks...moving across the country, finding out I was adopted...it was just making me come unhinged. It was the only way I could explain all of the weird things I'd seen and experienced lately.

I was having a mental breakdown in the place where I'd just taken a job.

Footsteps on the stairs behind me made my heart jump.

"...And don't you ever think you're being an imposition," I heard Aunt Candace say. "You are welcome at our table whenever you want. Bliss will even swing by and get you if you're having a harder time than usual getting around."

"You really are too kind, Candace," Abe said as the two of them appeared at the counter.

Fear flooded my veins, making my knees weak. Without thinking, I snatched the book out of the air, snapping it shut as I did. The blue glow disappeared, and the hum died away.

I hurriedly tucked the book away on the shelf, exactly where I'd found it.

Abe spotted me as I turned and headed back toward them, my heart in my throat.

He smiled. "I hope you're finding everything to your liking?" he asked.

"You have some real treasures here, Mr. Cromwell," I said. "I've never seen a more eclectic collection."

He beamed at me.

"Well, we should let Mr. Cromwell rest," Aunt Candace said, gently laying her hand on my shoulder.

"Thank you very much for the job offer," I told Mr. Cromwell as he walked with us to the door. "You have no idea how much I appreciate it."

He smiled again. "But of course. I think you will find some strange and unique things here."

He had no idea.

8

I squinted against the sunlight as we stepped out of the shop. I hadn't realized how dark it was inside.

I'll make sure it's cheerful and bright in there, too. We wouldn't want to scare customers away.

If I was honest, though, it wouldn't be the dirty windows and dusty shelves that scared them away. It'd be the strange floating books.

Stop it, Marianne. The book wasn't floating. You're just stressed.

Yeah, that was it.

I glanced out over the valley, taking in the view and pushing the weird book from my mind. I inhaled the sweet mountain air, heavy with the scent of pine and the faint remnants of smoke from a bonfire being burned somewhere nearby.

Across the valley nestled amongst the trees sat a stone structure. It caught my eye since it was such a contrast to the surrounding greens and browns of the trees, like a building carved from ice. It had towers arching straight into the sky.

A twinge of fear flooded me as the images from my

nightmares pushed into my mind. The tall walls of that structure reminded me of the old fort. Jacob's dead eyes staring into the darkness–

"Hey, Aunt Candace?" I asked while she unlocked her car as we walked toward it. I pointed out across the valley. "What's that place?"

She glanced in the direction I pointed, and I saw a flicker of fear pass over her face before she turned and smiled at me. "Oh, that's the old Blackburn castle. It's a little out of place, isn't it?"

I gazed at the castle. "Yeah. I didn't think there were actual castles in the US."

"That's because there aren't," she said. "Not in the truly old sense. This weird imitation of a medieval castle has been there for a long time, though. I guess the valley was sort of built around it. The Blackburns have lived there for many generations. Some say they used to be nobility from somewhere in Europe and came here to get away from persecution. Others have said they were oil barons and moved here to try and make a name for themselves when the gold rush happened. No one really knows for sure."

"Hasn't anyone asked them?" I wondered aloud.

"They keep to themselves for the most part," Aunt Candace said. "Some people say it's because they feel they're too good for us. But Bliss seems to think they just like their privacy."

The castle loomed in the distance. It seemed shrouded in secrets, like something out of a fairytale.

There was a scrape of shoes on the gravel behind me, and I glanced over my shoulder.

A tall man with a slate grey peacoat was walking toward the doors of Abe's shop. I saw a sleek red Ferrari parked just off to the side of Aunt Candace's car. I blinked. How had I not noticed him pull up? Or had he been there before we came outside?

I hadn't even heard the car pull into the lot.

"Come along, Marianne," Aunt Candace said, dropping her voice. "There are some things that I need to take care of back at the lodge."

The man glanced over his shoulder and spotted us. "Ah, Mrs. Brooks. What a pleasure." His voice was rich and deep, and he had an accent that I didn't recognize. It was silky and thick, and I found myself wanting to hear him speak again just so I could hear it.

He turned and I got a good look at him. He had a chiseled jawline where he sported a closely trimmed beard that was the same coppery red as his thick, windswept hair. It was well styled and yet looked effortless at the same time. As he approached, I noticed there were streaks of premature grey near his temples. And his eyes...they were like pools of liquid topaz, golden and mesmerizing.

I was startled by how attractive he was. He had to be at least in his late thirties, but he'd aged incredibly well. I'd always heard that about men, but he seemed to be the reason that saying was started in the first place.

A lump formed in my throat as he drew nearer.

"Ah, yes. Hello, Dr. Valerio," Aunt Candace said with a tight smile. I'd seen my mother use the same smile whenever she'd run into a passive aggressive neighbor that had lived at the end of our street. I was surprised to recognize it so easily.

He stopped in front of us and looked over at Abe's store. "I suppose the old man hasn't opened his fine establishment again yet?"

"Not yet," Aunt Candace said. "But it will be open again this coming Monday."

His handsome face split into a smile, and his golden eyes seemed to shine. "Splendid. I take it he's feeling well enough?"

Aunt Candace spared me a glance. "Well, he's hired some help. My niece here."

He turned his gaze to me, and a shiver ran down my spine.

"This is Marianne," Aunt Candace said. "Marianne, this is Dr. Valerio, the owner of the bank in town."

"It's a pleasure to meet you, Marianne," Dr. Valerio said, holding out his hand. "And might I say...you have the most striking eye color. They're like the sky before a storm."

My face flushed scarlet. I took his hand and shook it. His grip was strong, and his eyes never left mine. It was as if I was glued in place. "The pleasure is mine," I said, my voice quivering slightly. I removed my hand from his, and it was like I lost something. A memory, or a feeling of some sort. It was distant, like it was just on the outside of my periphery. "That accent," I said, desperate to move his focus off of me. "Is it French?"

"Italian," he said with an easy smile. It made my heart twinge in a strange way. "My parents were both from Rome, and I've spent a great deal of time there myself. Have you ever been?"

"No," I said, "But I'd love to one day."

His smile grew. "Italy is one of the prettiest countries in the world," he said. "And where do you hail from, Marianne? I cannot place your accent."

"I have an accent?" I asked, with a short laugh. "Missouri, but I was born here."

"Were you really?" he asked, and he leaned in, his eyes shining with interest. "I wish I was born here. This valley... it's my true home."

I swallowed nervously as I saw him surveying the landscape as if it belonged to him. By the look of his expensive suit and his wing-tipped shoes, I could easily imagine that he could buy every square mile of land without blinking.

He looked back at me and there was a glint of something mysterious in his eyes. It sent a chill down my spine and made me turn to look at my Aunt. "Well, it was really nice to meet you, Dr. Valerio, but my aunt and I need to be heading back to the lodge. I'm sure I'll see you around."

"Indeed you will," he said. "I tend to frequent Mr. Cromwell's shop in search of any kind of valuable artifacts. I look forward to getting to know you better, Marianne."

"Likewise," I said, red flags waving furiously in my mind. "See you later."

"Have a good afternoon," Aunt Candace said.

"Drive safely," Dr. Valerio called after us. "The wolves have been seen prowling near the roads just outside the town limits."

My ears burned, but I forced myself not to turn around. How weird that he'd mentioned wolves and I'd seen one that morning. Maybe it was just a friendly warning.

Something told me that he meant something more, though.

We hopped in the car, and Aunt Candace didn't waste any time pulling out of the small parking lot and back onto the main road.

We sat in silence for a few minutes. I stared out the window at the trees rushing past, nervousness keeping me quiet as I looked for another pair of golden eyes in the shadows.

Dr. Valerio's eyes had seemed so strange, so entrancing that I was sure I'd see them in my dreams that night.

"So what do you think about Abe and his shop?" my aunt asked eventually.

I perked up, grateful that she hadn't started with a question about Dr. Valerio. "Oh, I think that'll be great. It's completely different than anything I've ever done before, so I am going to welcome the change of pace."

She smiled as she slowed at a stop sign. "Good, I'm glad to hear it. I could see the relief on poor Abe's face. It will help him to rest, I think. And he needs to. That man tries to do too much."

Somehow I felt like she was dancing around something, and my stomach constricted when I thought about the book. For a half a second, I thought about asking her. It was like talking to my mother. But even I knew that I wouldn't admit to her that I'd been hearing foxes talking to me and seeing books float and glow like I'd cast some sort of spell.

I smirked. Yeah, right. A spell? That was ridiculous.

"...so she asked me if...Marianne?" Aunt Candace asked.

I straightened and looked over at her, my eyes wide as I realized she'd been talking while my mind drifted. "Yes?"

She sighed, but smiled kindly at me. "I'm sorry. You must be completely exhausted, aren't you?"

I smiled back. "Yeah, I guess I am. I just keep zoning out. I'm sorry, what were you saying?"

"I was just telling you a story about your mother," she said. "Why don't we head back to the lodge where we left your car and I'll make you something to eat? You can take whatever we have leftover home. I can't imagine you've had a chance to get over to the grocery store yet. Why don't I send Bliss to get some things for you? You could make a list for us and that way you can focus on unpacking."

My first reaction was to tell her no, that I was totally fine going and getting my own groceries. But then I realized I was basically so stressed I was hallucinating weird stuff, so really, it was probably better for me to drive as little as possible until I'd gotten enough rest. I could maybe even squeeze in a nap after I'd changed the sheets on my bed back at the cabin and taken another hot shower.

"That's really kind, Aunt Candace," I said. "And honestly, it would be a huge help. I'll pay for everything, of course. Just have her keep the receipts and I'll write you a check."

"Absolutely not," she said. "It's the least I can do for my niece who just moved here. You deserve to be showered in a little love when everything is so strange and new."

She wasn't wrong. Everything was strange and new. That was probably where all this uneasiness was coming from. I was out here on my own, barely knowing anyone or anything about the area in general. It was going to take time for this place to feel like home.

I needed some rest, and some time to explore and settle in. Once I became more familiar with my surroundings and didn't have to rely on my GPS anymore, I'd feel better. I knew I would.

I just wanted things to go back to normal.

But as I stared out at the moody forests, the branches of the trees swaying in the midafternoon wind, I could almost swear that the world I'd left and the world I'd entered were very different from one another.

It was better to keep the things I'd noticed to myself, at least for now. There was no sense making Aunt Candace worry that I might be losing my mind.

I just needed rest.

I'd look at that book again on Monday with fresh eyes, and prove to myself once and for all that things were normal around here.

9

Even though it was only the second time I'd stepped through the beautifully crafted wooden front doors of the lodge, it was incredibly comforting to recognize a place and to know it was safe. Bliss was there waiting for us, ready to inform her mother that it had taken effort, but she made sure that old Mr. Terrance went on his lunchbreak.

I ate dinner with the two of them, and I couldn't remember the last time I'd enjoyed a meal so much. We laughed and swapped stories. It seemed that Bliss and I were very similar to one another; we both loved being outdoors, preferred cats to dogs, and really loved the occasional deep fried chocolate cookie. Aunt Candace, however, was like a carbon copy of my mother. She moved her hands in the same way that Mom did when she spoke, and was frightened of frogs and lizards the same way she was. They had their differences, though. Aunt Candace, for one, really loved coffee, and my mom couldn't stand it. Mom also loved going for hikes. Aunt Candace preferred getting her exercise in the pool at the lodge.

I finally relaxed as we sat there enjoying the most delicious pumpkin pie I'd ever had in my life. The memories of the last few days seemed to fade away into the past, and I was feeling much more positive about the move. I was almost excited.

I compiled a list of things I wanted from the store, including bread, eggs, and my favorite English breakfast tea, and Bliss waved to us as she hopped in her car and drove off for me. I hoped I hadn't put too many things on there for her to get.

"Now, you are going to need something else to get around town with," Aunt Candace said, waving me on after her. We wandered around the outside of the lodge toward a large shed just inside the forest. She unlocked it with a key on the loop of hundreds she carried around. I was amazed she'd been able to find the right key among so many, as we stepped inside.

There was a lawn mower, some rock salt for the parking lot in the winter, and a number of mountain bikes on racks along one wall.

"This is how people in Faerywood Falls really get around," she said, pointing up at the bikes. "Especially around the lake. Old Abe's shop is only a few miles from here, so if you wanted to save some money on gas, you could ride one of these to work on the sunnier days."

I gazed up at the bikes. "I haven't ridden a bike since I was a kid," I said. "But I loved doing it when I did."

"There's a reason why everyone compares tasks you never forget to riding a bike," she said. "You can have your pick of these three here, if you want."

"You guys have been too generous," I said.

I ended up choosing a pretty turquoise blue bike with a

bell on it. Aunt Candace said that it had been Bliss's favorite bike for many years until she upgraded.

She asked a few of the guys working the landscape to come and help me attach the bike rack to the back of my car, which they managed to do in just a few minutes.

The sun was starting to set as Aunt Candace and I hoisted the bike up onto the rack, securing it there.

"All right, you should get home and get some rest," Aunt Candace said with a broad grin. "I'm sure you're just exhausted."

"I am," I admitted. "I didn't know moving took this much out of you."

"It's a big change, both physically and emotionally," Aunt Candace said. "Now, why don't you come over for lunch on Sunday? We're having prime rib."

My stomach rumbled even though I'd just eaten. "That sounds amazing."

"Good," she said with a smile and a nod. "Now go get some rest. We won't bother you tomorrow, I promise."

"You wouldn't be bothering me," I said as I opened my driver's side door.

Aunt Candace watched me from the front steps of the lodge as I drove off down the dirt road toward my cabin. There was a warm glow in my heart as I watched her fade away in my rearview mirror. I had come not knowing anyone, but I had family here, and it was as if I'd known them for years already.

The cabin was dark and quiet as I approached, the evening sun reflecting off the windows in bright reds and oranges. I gazed out over the lake, relishing the view that was just outside my front door. It was stunning, and I wasn't sure I'd ever been more proud to live in a place, no matter how tiny.

I rubbed my eyes as I grabbed a box out of the backseat, deciding that now was as good a time as any to start unpacking the back of the car. It was heavy, and I saw I'd labeled it *kitchen* in obnoxious pink marker. Pots and pans probably. Or my extensive mug collection.

I trudged up the stairs, digging through my purse with one hand while trying to deftly balance the box on my hip with the other. I managed to locate my keys just before the box toppled out of my hands and onto the steps.

I slid the lock home, pushed open the door, and stepped inside. I set the box down on the narrow countertop just beside the door, and froze.

I wasn't alone in the cabin. A tiny red and white face stared up at me from the couch. A pair of black eyes blinked at me, and a little black nose twitched.

I was glad I'd put the box down, otherwise it would have gone careering out of my hands and smashed against the floor.

I peered at the fox, all curled up in the blanket I'd nestled it in the night before. I'd ditched the box that morning after talking to the vet, but the animal somehow managed to find the blanket folded up on the arm of the sofa.

How had it gotten back in? I'd closed all the windows on my way out, afraid of soaking the whole inside if it started to rain in my absence. I glanced around and my eyes fell on a doggie door no bigger than a foot and a half tall in the wall beside the front door. The perfect size for a fox to squeeze through.

"Well, aren't you a clever little thing?" I said hesitantly, walking inside, but giving the fox a wide berth. The vet had given me very clear instructions to keep my distance from the fox in case it was carrying diseases. The last thing I needed was to drag myself down to the emergency room to get a rabies shot.

I never broke eye contact with the creature, thinking that if I did, it might show some kind of weakness or submission.

The fox's tail waved like a cat's, and a shiver ran down my spine. Hopefully the little creature wasn't agitated.

Why had it come back? What was it about my place that had seemed preferable to the outside, where it belonged?

I thought of the torn food container this morning and groaned.

This is why they tell you not to feed the birds at amusement parks, I thought. *They become dependent on you for food.*

Still...I worried about the fox's leg. Was it still hurting? Had it sought shelter in a safe place where it could heal?

I sighed, rubbing my hands over my face. How much harm could it really do? I had slept with it in the same room all night, for Pete's sake. If it wanted to attack me, it would have done it then, right?

I was making excuses with myself, and I really couldn't be sure why. The smartest thing to do was to call the vet back and ask for his help, but something kept me from reaching for my phone to call him.

Would it really harm anything to give it just a little more food? Maybe that would give the fox enough strength to leave. As soon as it was gone, I'd block the doggie door so it couldn't come back in. I'd call Mrs. Bickford tomorrow and ask her to send her handyman out to permanently board up the dog door. Then the fox would have no choice but to go back to the wild.

That seemed like the wisest thing. At least that was what I kept telling myself.

Making sure not to turn my back to the fox, who was still very comfortably seated on the blanket, watching me steadily, I went to the fridge and pulled out some milk. I then moved to the box near the door and picked up some of the roasted chicken that Aunt Candace had sent home with me.

I filled up a plastic cup with the milk, and set some chicken slices on a plate before putting it on the floor between the fox and me.

The fox looked up at me, and then down to the food before hopping down and slowly making its way over to the meal.

I watched it hesitantly. It was like watching a child eat. I was nervous and interested all at the same time.

The fox sniffed at the chicken before looking up at me.

This human is kind to me.

I blinked.

"Who said that?" I asked, turning and looking around. The front door was open, but my porch was empty. And I was the only one in that tiny, one room cabin besides...

I looked back at the fox, who had started gnawing on the chicken rather exuberantly.

My eyes narrowed as I looked at the creature.

That was twice now that I'd experienced this. There was no way. It was impossible.

I opened my mouth and then snapped it shut. No. I was not going to talk to a fox like it could understand me.

It's not like it would respond anyway. I really am losing my mind.

I would respond, if you spoke to me.

I jumped, nearly out of my skin, and collided with the small table and chairs behind me.

I clutched at my heart, staring down at the fox, who spared me nothing more than a brief glance before it started to lap at the milk in the red plastic cup. My heart thundered in my ears, and I squeezed my eyes shut.

This is a dream. It has to be.

Well, if you are dreaming, then I must be as well, for I can hear your thoughts as clearly as you hear mine.

I opened my eyes and looked down at the fox. "Are you saying..." I mumbled, sinking down into the chair behind me. "That...you can understand me?"

The fox raised its head and looked me dead in the eye. It sat back on its haunches, its front paws together in a very picturesque manner, and wrapped its tail around its body.

Yes, I can. And it seems you can understand me, as well.

My jaw dropped, and my hands covered my mouth in shock.

"How...this isn't possible. It can't be real – "

It seems very real to me, the fox said, blinking at me, tilting its head to the side. *Although you are the first human I've spoken with like this. Then again, perhaps you are a special kind of human.*

"No," I said, getting up and walking away. "This is just another part of my breakdown. That's all there is too it. I'm hearing voices in my head and think it's the fox sitting on my living room floor eating chicken leftovers."

I pressed my fingers against my temples, willing the insanity to work itself out of my brain.

"I am a normal, sane person. I'm just over exhausted, and dealing with some major life changes. Anyone is bound to go a little unhinged during all this stress. Right?" I asked to the air.

The fox blinked at me again, apparently unperturbed by my distress. *What if this is not so simply explained away?* The fox asked. *What if, instead, this is all real?*

I blanched, looking over at the tiny creature.

What if...what if the fox was right?

"Oh, good, you're home."

My heart stopped as I whirled around, knocking the stack of plastic cups off the table in the process.

Mrs. Bickford was standing there in the doorway, hands on her hips, still sporting that beekeeper's hat.

"Mrs. Bickford," I said, clasping my hands over my heart, my breathing coming in shallow gasps. "You startled me."

"Sorry about that," she said, strolling inside as if it were her own place. I guessed it was, but it would have been nice if she'd knocked. "I just forgot to tell you this morning that the cabin doesn't have a washer and dryer, but that the laundromat for the whole lake is just a half a mile from the lodge up on the hill," she said. "I know that's a big inconvenience for some people, but the washer only costs a quarter, and the dryer is ten cents. Just keep your pocket change whenever you get groceries and you'll be fine."

"Okay, thanks for the advice," I said, still clutching at my heart, willing it to slow down.

"Still unpacking, huh?" she asked, staring at the box on the counter. "I saw you still had a pretty full vehicle, too, when I walked by."

A twinge of annoyance vibrated in my head, but I shoved it aside, smiling at her instead.

"And eating on the floor, I see," Mrs. Bickford said, staring down at the plate and plastic cup on the floor.

Remembering her rule against animals in the cabin, I looked down nervously. The fox –

It was nowhere in sight.

"Going for that whole low carb diet, huh?" said Mrs. Bickford. "Well, protein always does the body good. Just don't forget to let yourself indulge once in a while. Life's too short to deny yourself some cake. Or some spaghetti Bolognese." She turned and looked beside her as if someone was standing there. "You know as well as I do that my Bolognese is better. No, don't you give me that look, mister."

"Um...is everything okay?" I asked, fear starting to make the little hairs on my arm stand up.

Mrs. Bickford rolled her eyes and gestured to the thin air beside her. "It's my husband, Jim. Even as a ghost, he can't admit that my Bolognese was better than his. Typical man, am I right?"

"Your husband is a...ghost?" I asked hesitantly, wondering if I should be calling Aunt Candace. I knew she and Bliss had told me my landlady was harmless, but that didn't mean it wasn't creeping me out.

Mrs. Bickford nodded, her fists remaining firmly planted on her hips. "Yes, but that doesn't stop him from still being a pain in my foot, does it? Now he can bother me at any hour, and since he doesn't need to sleep or eat, it gives him extra time to try to tell me how to do my job." She turned her gaze back to the air. "Yes, I know you mean well, dear. I just think you should find a hobby or something else to do. I could handle these inspections before, and I still can."

I swallowed nervously.

"Well, I won't keep you. I just wanted to make sure I passed that little bit of information along," Mrs. Bickford said with a smile that I wasn't sure was entirely genuine. "Did you have any questions for me while I'm here?"

I glanced briefly at the doggie door. "No, that's everything, I think. If I think of anything, I'll be sure to come and find you."

"No problem," Mrs. Bickford said. "You have a great night, Marianne."

"You as well, Mrs. Bickford," I said, following her out to the porch.

"I had that last night, dear," Mrs. Bickford said to the air beside her, glowering. "I'm in no mood for indigestion this late in the day."

I rolled my eyes and turned around, heading back inside. "She's a few screws short of a hardware store..." I muttered under my breath.

In reality, though, I didn't have any room to talk, did I? I was talking with a fox before Mrs. Bickford barged in here without notice. With my mind.

I collapsed on the couch, scrubbing at my forehead with my fingers.

If I was willing to entertain the idea that I was communicating with a fox, then I should also be prepared to believe that the older woman really *could* see her dead husband's ghost.

My head collapsed onto the cushion behind me, and I groaned.

She is a peculiar one, isn't she?

I flinched, but at least I didn't tumble out of the couch. Maybe my surprise receptors were overtaxed at that point. I opened one eye and saw that the fox had come out of hiding, and was perched on the arm of the couch, watching me steadily as its tail swung back and forth behind it.

I lifted my head, giving the fox a good look over. "All right. If you and I somehow share this...connection that we seem to have, I guess it's only polite that we introduce ourselves. My name is Marianne. What's yours?"

The fox blinked. *I do not have a name in the same way that you do.*

I chewed on the inside of my lip. "Well, you'll need a name so I can call you something instead of 'Fox'."

Would you care to give me one?

I fixed my gaze on the tiny creature. "I...I guess I could. I don't know anything about you, though."

Do humans not name their pets when they bring them into their homes? The fox asked.

"No, they do," I said. I frowned. "I wouldn't necessarily think of you as a pet, though. You're...different."

Is it I who is different, or you? The fox asked, its tail swinging.

I was caught off guard by that question. "I...I don't know. I mean, I guess I could be different. Everything has been so weird since I got to Faerywood Falls."

Then perhaps something has changed in you that has allowed you to hear my thoughts, the fox mused. It was almost as if I could hear a purr. Did foxes purr? *I know that I am no different than I was before we met. Can you say the same?*

"No, I guess I can't." I said.

Suddenly I remembered the woman at the gas station with the squirrel on her shoulder, and the raccoon in the nest behind the counter. She seemed completely content with them.

Almost in the same way I was with this fox, now.

"You don't think..." I said, my brow furrowing. "That other people around here can talk to animals, too...do you?"

The fox blinked slowly at me. *There have been stranger things to happen in this forest. Did you meet someone like that?*

I quickly explained about the woman at the gas station. "When I accidentally touched her, there was like this pulse that ran down my spine, almost like a shock or something. I would've written it off as static electricity, but it was way different than that. Something more."

Do you think she somehow passed this ability on to you? The fox asked.

"Well, maybe," I said. "I mean, before that, I definitely

couldn't talk to animals. But then I find you, and then we can communicate…" I glanced out the window. "I wonder if I can only talk to you, or if there are other animals I could try talking to."

There is only one way to find out, the fox said.

"I suppose you're right…" I said. But I couldn't find the strength to pull myself off the couch and go out looking for a bird or frog to talk to. I also didn't have the courage to admit that something could have actually happened to me, giving me this…ability? Power? I didn't know what to think of it.

I never thanked you, the fox said, lifting one of its black footed paws and licking it lazily. *For saving me last night. It was a very heroic thing to have done.*

"I couldn't just leave you there on the side of the road," I said. "I never would have forgiven myself."

I am humbled by your kindness, the fox said. *Most humans would think nothing of leaving me there.*

"Well, your perception of humanity seems pretty dead on," I said, stretching my arms up over my head before letting out a long exhale and collapsing back into the cushions. "All right, so you need a name. Well, first things first, are you male or female?" I asked.

The fox tilted its head to the side. *Female, of course. I thought that much was obvious.*

"Sorry," I said. "I'm still new to foxes in general. I've only ever admired your kind from a distance. All right, so let's try a few. What about…Red?" I asked.

If she could have arched an eyebrow at me, I thought she would have.

"Too general?" I asked, nodding. "Okay. What about…Lily?"

As in the flower? She asked. *I think not.*

"Okay, no inspiration from nature, then."

We continued like this for some time, trying to find the right name for her. She didn't like any of them, and it was well after dark when we'd settled in. I'd spent a few hours hauling things from my car to the cabin, all the while volleying names to the fox for approval.

"You know, you are awfully opinionated for someone who doesn't know what they want their name to be," I said. "You didn't like flower names, or names based out of books. I even tried some more ethereal names. None of them suited you."

None of them rang true to me, she said. *I simply wish to find the most reasonable one.*

"Reasonable," I said, combing through a box I'd tucked onto one of the rickety kitchen chairs. I found my tea kettle and yanked it out. "You sound like the Greek goddess Athena. I did a project about her in fifth grade. She was supposed to be ruled by her reason, and often would forget about her emotions and compassion for others because of it."

*Athena...*the fox said. *I rather like the sound of that.*

I rolled my eyes and turned to her. "Really? Out of all the names we talked about, you pick the one I just happen to mention in passing?"

You yourself said that I resemble her in a way, the fox said. Her tail flicked and wrapped around herself. *Yes. I like Athena.*

I sighed, but smirked at her as I filled my tea kettle. "Very well, then. Athena it is."

10

Monday came too quickly. It always did, but after spending all weekend unpacking boxes and finding creative places to store my belongings in the tiny cabin, I felt like I hadn't gotten any rest at all. The most relaxing time I'd had was when I'd gone for dinner at the lodge, enjoying another delicious meal prepared by Bliss.

Athena hadn't been unhappy to stay home then, but as I packed a backpack with a few things I'd need for my first day of work, she hopped up onto the seat of the bicycle and blinked at me. *I'm going with you,* she said.

"What? Why?" I asked.

Well, whatever this magic is that connects us –

"It's not magic," I said for the hundredth time. "It's... something else."

Athena sniffed in annoyance. *Whatever it may be, it draws me to you, and I feel less anxious when we are together. Besides, what are you going to do all day in that big shop all by yourself?*

"Work," I said, clipping my helmet underneath my chin. "Like any good employee should."

I soon realized there was no arguing with her. She was bullheaded and much faster than I gave her credit for, because she'd hopped into my backpack and settled in while my back was turned as I was filling my thermos with coffee.

I found her and could only sigh. "All right, but you can't be seen," I said.

That won't be a problem, she said.

I'd ridden the bike back and forth to the lodge, but hadn't realized just how out of practice with riding a bike I really was. It left my muscles sore and aching, numbing everything from my hips down. The antique shop wasn't all that far away, but part of it was uphill, which meant I was walking next to the bike, gripping onto it for dear life as I panted and wiped sweat from my forehead.

Athena seemed to be enjoying herself when we were actually riding, though. She'd peek her head out of the bag and sniff at the air like a dog, squinting against the wind and sun.

I liked having her company. I'd never really had a pet of my own as a kid. Mom was so allergic to cats that she'd swell up like a sausage if we ever visited family that owned any, and she'd been bitten by a dog when she was young and so she didn't like them.

Athena was different, though. She fended for herself, for the most part, but insisted that I still give her milk when she came in for the night. I had found her lying in patches of warm afternoon sunlight more than once in the few days we'd been living together, and she still didn't know that I'd recognized the weight and warmth against my legs in the middle of the night as her way of being affectionate.

I parked my bike around the back of the shop and walked around to the front, using the great big key that Abe had given me to unlock the door. Athena's whiskers tickled my face as she peered over my shoulder.

This place has an interesting presence, she said.

"What do you mean by that?" I asked. I knew that she could hear my thoughts sometimes, but we still hadn't really learned how to do that well yet.

I'm not sure. It's familiar, but it's almost like it has a life of its own, she said. *It must be the magic.*

"What did I say about using the word magic?" I asked as I unlocked the door and stepped inside.

Just because you won't admit it exists doesn't mean it doesn't, she retorted.

I groaned.

It was dim inside, even after I'd switched the lights on. I noticed a few bulbs had burned out, and more than one light fixture had spiderwebs hanging inside.

After I went up and said good morning to Mr. Cromwell, I located the cleaning supplies in the narrow closet behind the counter and began to work. I wanted the shop in some semblance of order before I reopened it.

Athena located a shelf in the middle of the store and perched on top of it, watching me as I swept the floors, dusted the surfaces, and scrubbed at the windows. It was only noon before I took a step back and admired my work.

"It already looks better in here," said a voice near the stairs.

I whirled around and saw Abe standing there, a perfectly content smile spreading up his face.

"You've done a magnificent job, young lady," he said, peering at me over his spectacles. "I really don't know how I can thank you."

I smiled back at him. "I'm happy to do it, Mr. Cromwell.

This is a welcome difference to my hectic job as an accountant."

"That's what your aunt said," Mr. Cromwell said. "Well, why don't we flip that open sign and let the world know we are back open for business?"

I walked over to the window, and after giving the sign a much needed wipe with the cloth in my hand, flipped it around.

"And now...we wait," Mr. Cromwell said, his smile growing wider.

The first few hours were a little slow, but I hadn't really expected anything else. I didn't think we'd get any customers the first day being open. I remembered that Dr. Valerio mentioned he would stop by, but hadn't said when.

Mr. Cromwell sat down in a chair behind the counter, clearly wanting to see the revival of his business with his own eyes.

I wasn't surprised that Athena had made herself scarce. When I tried to reach out to her with my mind, I realized I must have been the one struggling to make the connection, and not her. It made me start to think about whether or not distance would affect our communication, too. The whole thing was so strange to me still that I figured it was better to just go along with it than try to reason it out.

Every time I thought about my new ability, though, I kept going back to that woman at the gas station. That had to be the source of it. I had no other reasonable explanation.

I continued to sweep and dust until I was content that no one would have a sneezing fit when they stepped inside, and set about rearranging some of the items. I tried to organize them by type, and if I couldn't, I tried to arrange them by time period. Mr. Cromwell had a nice arrangement of early twentieth century chairs, and I put them all together with a table and a tea set in a corner, as if inviting the customers over for an afternoon of elegance.

Mr. Cromwell seemed thrilled at the changes. "I like your spunk, kid," is what he told me.

We'd had three customers before I found I was brave enough to approach the bookshelf in the back. I hadn't gone near it since I'd found that red leather book when I'd come here with my aunt.

The curiosity was too strong, though. I had to look at it again.

Mr. Cromwell had excused himself to go take some of his afternoon medicine, and the store was empty.

I made my way over to the shelf with a duster in hand, intending to look busy if any new customers appeared. Part of me hoped they wouldn't walk in if the book decided it wanted to hover above my hands again. I didn't feel like trying to explain something that I hardly understood myself.

I pulled the book off the shelf and flipped it open. It looked the same as I remembered, with glimmering blue letters that seemed to shift and change, and were in no particular order.

Is this the book you were telling me about?

I whirled around, looking near my feet, but didn't see Athena anywhere.

Up here.

I looked up and saw her lying on top of some satin drapery. Her tail flicked lazily behind her, and her front paws were crossed.

"Yeah," I said, willing my now racing heart to slow. "I just wanted to look at it again."

You said it floated last time, right?

"When I said a certain word, yeah," I said. "The only

thing is, I can't remember what that word was. It started with an R, I remember that much."

Maybe try saying a few words, see if it works again, Athena suggested.

I did, but nothing happened.

I even flipped to the part of the book where the letters changed from blue to red. None of them made any sense, though.

"They're changing so fast I can't read anything," I said, squinting at the page. "Maybe I just imagined the whole thing, after all."

That's what you thought about hearing me, though, Athena said. *I don't think you would have imagined something so clearly.*

She was probably right.

"Oh, here's something," I said, tracing my finger down the page. Some of the letters seemed to have stabilized. "I can almost read it...*Fro...sen...tia?*"

I stared at the book, but there was no glowing, no humming, no indication that anything had happened.

"Well, that definitely wasn't the same word I spoke the other day," I said.

Marianne, look!

I lifted my head to Athena, who was now standing, her nose pointing in a direction over my head.

I looked up and saw an antique clock sitting on the top shelf of the bookcase. The golden face of the clock was starting to cloud over, and it took me a second to realize that it was, in fact, frosting over.

I stared at it, open mouthed.

Streaks of ice covered the glass, and I could hear it cracking and snapping as if it were below zero in the room.

*Marianne, you should move...*Athena said.

"Why?" I asked.

Just move –

I ducked just as the face of the clock shattered, spraying glass and gears outward into the store.

I looked down at the book in my hands, putting the two together, and snapped it shut, hefting it up onto a nearby table.

"What was that?" Mr. Cromwell called from the top of the stairs. "Did I just hear glass breaking?"

"Yes, Mr. Cromwell, I'm sorry," I said, getting to my feet and brushing the bits of glass from the front of my shirt. "I was cleaning and this clock...it just shattered."

"Was it the one with the little dancing people?" he asked.

I took a closer look at the remains of the clock. "No," I said.

"All right, that's good," he said. "No harm done. It was bound to happen at some point."

"Yeah, but not on my first day..." I said under my breath.

The tiny bell above the door chimed as the door opened, and three people stepped inside.

"Welcome," I said with a broad smile. "Please be careful if you come over here. One of our clocks broke. I was just cleaning it up."

"Oh, good heavens," said an elderly woman with a blue net hat on. "Do be careful with that glass."

I went to the back and pulled the broom out of the closet, along with the small handheld vacuum. I saw Athena slip inside the closet before I closed the door. Probably best while customers were around.

I swept up the shards, my heart pounding all the while. First the book floated, and then it...what...coated the whole clock in ice somehow? It definitely seemed to respond whenever I read the words off the page out loud. But if I were to open the book again, I would bet that particular word wouldn't be there anymore.

I knelt down with the vacuum to get the last few sparkling shards off the ground when a pair of blue and yellow striped stockings appeared in my periphery. I glanced up and saw a woman in a short navy dress peering down at a small, carved end table.

"I'm sorry, ma'am," I said. "But there might be some broken glass nearby, so please watch your – "

My jaw fell open as I saw her lift the red leather book and open it right up.

The vacuum clattered onto the floor as I jumped to my feet and snatched the book out of the woman's hands. "Again, I'm terribly sorry, but this book is not for sale," I said.

The woman looked up at me. She had vibrantly purple eyes, a thin pointed nose with a pointed chin to match, and dirty blonde hair with the ends dyed blue. Her pencil thin eyebrows shot upward with indignation as I tucked the book underneath my arm. Her look of shock quickly melted into one of sickly sweetness, though. "Would you be willing to negotiate?" she asked. "That book looks quite intriguing, and I would be oh so interested in adding it to my collection of fascinating books."

Her voice was like tar covered in honey. Her eyes glinted as they fixed on the book instead of my face.

"I'm really sorry, but this is just not for sale," I said, moving past the woman and walking toward the counter with the book. It was my fault, really, for leaving it out in the open like that where anyone could find it.

"Then why was it out in the store among everything else that is for sale?" the woman asked, a bite to her words, though it was clear she was trying to remain civil.

I put the book carefully behind the counter. "That was my mistake," I said. "I've been trying to get everything cleaned up in here for Mr. Cromwell, and I neglected to put everything where it belonged when I should have. Really, I am sorry."

The woman huffed, tossing her hair over her shoulder. "I have never been treated so unfairly in all my life," she said, her eyes narrowing. She jabbed a finger in my direction. "You listen here, missy. You tell Mr. Cromwell that he is going to regret not selling me that book."

"Mr. Cromwell has nothing to do with it," I said, my heart in my throat. I was starting to fear challenging this woman. But I couldn't just let her walk out of here with a book that seemed to have the capability of setting clocks off like explosive icicles. That would be incredibly dangerous.

And if I was honest with myself, there was a part of me that wanted to see what the book was really capable of for myself...

"We also do not appreciate threats in this store," I said, my hands shaking behind the counter. "So I am going to have to ask you to leave."

The woman's gaze turned dark. "Oh, I'll leave all right. Leave and take my money with me. You won't see me walk through this door ever again!" she declared as she stomped between the shelves toward the door. She yanked the heavy wood open, and then slammed it behind her, making a tremor run down the length of the room.

The two older women who were standing off to the side turned to look at me with concern. "Are you all right, dear?"

I took a shaky breath, but nodded. "Yeah, I'm fine. I'm sorry about that."

"You have nothing to apologize for," said the other

woman. "Some people are just so selfish that they can't handle it when things don't go their way."

"Yeah..." I said, my eyes lingering on the door. "People are selfish...aren't they?"

My fingers touched the cover of the red book, and I felt a protectiveness wash over me. It wasn't selfishness, not really. It was to keep other people safe.

At least that was what I kept telling myself.

11

I had never liked any of the retail jobs I'd had in high-school and college. They were always at the local shopping mall or at some fast food restaurant. They were stressful and boring all at the same time. I'd learned early on that I was good with numbers, and even better when it came to managing money, and so not only would I get told to do the bookkeeping at those low paying jobs, I also decided I should make a career out of it. Four years of college later, I left with a degree in hand and debt up to my eyeballs.

I worked as an accountant for seven years after that. My days were all sort of the same, and it wasn't long before the work lost its charm. I didn't love my job, but I didn't hate it, either. I knew that in that regard, I was better off than most.

Working at Abe's Antiques completely changed my mind about the matter. I found that I could do the book-keeping side of things as well as manage inventory, deciding what was worth keeping at the store to sell, and what wasn't. It gave me a chance to do some research about the objects we received, and learn the history of some of the items.

The only thing that had really stumped me so far was the book. I couldn't seem to find anything about it online anywhere.

There were a few other pieces that seemed a little...off when they came into the donation boxes. Things I couldn't find information on, either.

Athena and I had developed a bit of a routine, which was helping me get adjusted to my new life in Faerywood Falls. Every morning we'd wake up around six. We'd go for a run together by the lake. We'd come back, and I'd shower while she napped. We'd have breakfast together; something healthy and hearty for me while she ate whatever she'd found in the forest nearby.

Then we'd hop on the bike and head to the store, where we'd spend most of the day.

And I was really starting to love it.

It was the Saturday of my second full week working at the store. I'd spent a good portion of the afternoon with Abe going over some of the more detailed information about the budgeting.

"Now, you make sure you enjoy your day tomorrow, all right?" Abe said. "I'm glad that I keep the store closed at least one day a week. Otherwise you'd never take a break, would you?"

I grinned at him. "I really like working here."

"Yes, but you'll burn yourself out eventually," he said. "Look at me. I love this shop, too, but I should have given myself a chance to live my life outside of it. Now, go on. I'll see you on Monday, all right?"

I said goodbye to Mr. Cromwell and made my way back downstairs.

Athena had fallen asleep on my jacket, which she'd pulled down onto the chair and curled up in.

I was just packing my backpack when I heard a rumble of thunder outside.

Athena perked her head up.

"Oh, great," I said, deflating. "I should have checked the weather this morning. I hope we can make it home before it rains."

"Be careful out there," Abe called as he started down the stairs to the shop. "You get going. Don't worry about locking up; I can take care of that."

I waved Athena into the backpack, where she disappeared just before Abe appeared through the black curtains. "Thanks, Mr. Cromwell. You take it easy, okay?"

"If it starts raining, just pull over and give your aunt a call, okay?" he said.

"Will do," I said, pulling my hood up over my head.

The sky was becoming awfully ominous as I mounted the bike. It wasn't a far trip back to the cabin, but I wasn't liking the look of the rolling clouds overhead.

They're moving fast, Athena commented. I saw her little nose peek out over the top of my backpack, sniffing the air. *The clouds, I mean. We'd better hurry.*

"You don't have to tell me twice," I said, setting my feet on the pedals and starting to move.

I hurried down the hills, careful to keep my hands on the brakes. The sky seemed to be chasing me, as if it were taunting me. It would win, and I knew it.

Thunder rumbled overhead, and my heart leapt into my throat.

How much further? Athena asked.

I wasn't sure, but I thought I could hear some anxiousness, even through her mind.

"Not far," I said, slowing to a stop at a stoplight. The

crossing sign across the street flashed orange, warning me not to walk. There were a few cars crossing, their headlights already on despite the early hour of the day. It was as if it was two or three hours later than it really was, given the darkness that had fallen over the valley. "We just have to cross Spruce Street here, and then head down along route 4..."

A crack of lightning lit up the sky in the direction that we had to ride.

I gulped.

The crossing sign changed, and I rode across the street, my heart beating uncomfortably in my chest. The inside of my cheek was raw from biting down on it.

We made our way down the road, and as we crested a low hill, I could see the lake in the distance.

Pure relief washed through me, and I smiled despite my exhaustion from pushing myself harder than normal. "We're almost there, Athena. I can see the lake."

Wonderful, the fox said. *And so far, no rain.*

Encouraged, I kept pushing myself along.

The only problem I found was that even though I'd seen the lake, it was still a few miles away. I was going to have to ride this road way around the outside of the lake, which ultimately was going to go right past my cabin. If only there was a shortcut...

There were walking trails through the woods though, weren't there? Aunt Candace had told me about them. I'd even seen one that came out right behind Mrs. Bickford's place.

That meant it connected to the forest that I was riding beside. It would cut the rest of our ride in half, and probably help get us home before it started to pour.

Thunder clapped overhead, causing me to twist the bike

handles. I nearly toppled off onto the pavement as a car raced past.

I pushed my helmet back up onto my head; it had fallen down over my eyes. I set my jaw. "That's it, we're taking a shortcut."

Athena appeared over my shoulder. *Shortcut? Where?*

I pointed to the tree line. I could see a sign for the hiking trails. "I have a mountain bike. They're made for that kind of terrain. Besides, it will keep us dry if it starts to rain before we get home."

Athena ducked back inside the backpack.

I turned the bike off the road and headed into the grass. The tires rumbled underneath me, but I was able to keep the wheels steady in the muddy earth.

I was amazed how smoothly it rode through the terrain. It wasn't all that much different than the tarmac. The paths, which were mostly dirt and rocks, were a bit harder to navigate, and I stopped just inside the line of trees. Darkness had fallen in earnest over the forest, and hardly any light made its way through the tall and ancient branches.

I took a deep breath. I could still see, and these trails were safe. And more than anything, I just wanted to get home.

I continued to push forward, finding it much harder to avoid the gaping holes in the ground as I rode. I kept my grip strong on the handlebars, and tried not to let my teeth chatter too much, worried I might accidentally bite the tip of my tongue off.

The trail meandered through the thick trees, and shadows greeted me at every turn. The smell of wet earth was strong, and thunder continued to rumble overhead.

A bat suddenly burst out from one of the trees, screeching as it went.

I let out a yelp of fear in response, and my hands wobbled on the handlebars. My front tire caught a sizable hole, and the bike flopped over onto the ground, taking me with it. I landed on my side, even though I'd tried to jump away as it tumbled over.

Pain shot up my leg as it tangled with the metal frame of the bike. Dread weighted my stomach as I tried my best to pull myself away, the back wheel spinning lazily in the air behind me.

Are you all right? Athena asked. She had managed to get out of the backpack before we fell over.

"I...I don't know," I said, shoving the bike off my legs. It scraped through the dirt, leaving streaks of mud on the frame. "My ankle...it really hurts." My hands trembled as I reached down to peel back my sock to examine the injury. I could touch it, even though it was incredibly tender.

Can you move it? Athena asked, walking around me slowly and sniffing at the area around my leg.

Wincing, I slowly rolled my ankle in a circle. It made my eyes water, and I had to remind myself to keep breathing. The pain was sharp and intense, but I could move it. "Well..." I said through gritted teeth. "I don't think it's broken."

What should we do? Athena asked.

I really didn't know. I looked up and down the path. My cabin was only a short distance away, maybe no more than a mile or so, but there was no way I was going to be able to walk there. Not with this pain.

"Can you grab my cell phone out of my backpack?" I asked. "I need to call my aunt."

Cell phone? Athena asked, looking up at me, her black eyes shining in the dim light. *You mean that pink and black box you talk into sometimes?*

"Yeah," I said, stretching the ankle out straight, trying to keep it steady.

It wasn't in there, Athena said.

"What?" I asked, my heart skipping. "It has to be. I was charging it and – " It was like someone knocked the wind out of my sails. "...I left it plugged into the charger, didn't I? What was I thinking?" I sighed, rubbing my hand over my face.

*I'm sorry there's nothing I can do...*Athena said, looking at me with sad eyes.

"It's all right," I said. "Maybe I just need a second to recover my strength."

The gentle pitter patter of rain started over our heads, the drops bouncing off the leaves of the branches high above. I looked up, and a few rogue drops managed to make it through the leaves, and flecked my cheeks and the ground around me.

I glanced over my shoulder and saw that a sturdy pine tree was directly behind me, its branches draped around the forest floor like a tent. That would probably be the driest place to wait out the pain.

I gathered my resolve, and pushed myself a few inches backward with my hands. The pain was bearable, and it was only in that one ankle.

I glowered down at it. "We were so close, too..."

Athena suddenly perked up, her snout pointed further down the path. She stood perfectly still, staring into the darkness.

"What is it?" I whispered.

*Something's out there...*she said.

I followed her gaze, and a shadowed silhouette stepped out from behind a fir tree. My heart skipped. "Oh my gosh, thank goodness someone walked by," I said. "I twisted my ankle. Do you by any chance have a cell phone on you? I need to call my aunt. She's the one who owns the lodge up on the hill – "

But the silhouette suddenly dissolved into a dark cloud with a bat-like shape and took off into the trees, disappearing.

My stomach dropped. "What...what was that?"

Athena hadn't relaxed. Her nose still pointed in the direction of the shadow.

I took a shuddering breath, the fear washing away some of the pain in my leg as I pushed myself all the way back against the trunk of the pine tree, its branches shielding me from the rain that started to fall more steadily overhead.

Athena hopped up onto my lap and spun around three times before settling down, her warmth a soothing presence.

I lay my head back against the tree and sighed. This place just kept getting weirder and weirder.

12

T he next thing I knew, it was pitch black out. At first, when I opened my eyes, I thought maybe I had gone blind. Panic flooded through me as I tried to move, but the pain in my ankle and the fallen pine needles jabbing into my palms reminded me where I was.

Athena stirred on my lap. *What's the matter?*

My mouth had gone dry. "We fell asleep. In the middle of the forest."

*That's not such a bad thing...*Athena said, laying her head back on my lap.

I wondered what time it was. Now that I stared in front of me, shapes started to appear in the darkness. It was quiet, too, aside from the hum of crickets. The rain had stopped. I could just make out the parting of the branches of the pine tree I sat against. My bike was still lying on the path, cast aside like a forgotten toy.

There was a sudden glow outside along the path. A small burst of warm green light, no bigger than my fingernail. It faded out of existence just as quickly as it had appeared.

I watched closely. Another green light appeared, and soon, a few others.

"Fireflies..." I said.

A few more began to glow, filling the path with a very dim light.

One of the fireflies came floating into the tent of pine branches. It lit up for a few seconds, long enough for me to watch its path across to me, and then it landed on my arm.

"Well, hello there," I said.

A strange sense of peace came over me. I didn't have to be scared of this forest. I wasn't sure how I knew that, especially with the creepy shadowy silhouette I'd seen earlier, but somehow I understood that it was safe.

There is magic about... Athena said.

I could feel a strange presence in the air, too. It was mingled with that peace I was feeling. It was almost like the memory of a voice I hadn't heard in a long time, or the echo of a warm hug that I'd been missing. It felt strangely familiar, as if I'd been here in this same place once before.

I tested my ankle, and realized that even if it was painful, I could move it easier now. I wondered if it might support my weight.

Be careful, Athena said, hopping down off me. *Don't push yourself too much.*

"I know," I said. "I just want to see these fireflies..."

Mom had said that they'd found me in a basket in the forest outside the lodge. This was that same forest, wasn't it? What did this place know about me and my past? What secrets did it hold about my life, and where I'd come from?

I hobbled out from underneath the branches, my sneakers scraping against the dead pine needles and fallen twigs. I probably wouldn't be able to walk with my injury for long, but with the help of my bike to support some of my weight, I would likely be able to make it home, now.

As I turned to look down the path, the fireflies had grown in numbers. Hundreds of them glimmered along the path, lighting the way through the darkness.

"It's almost as if..." I mumbled, staring dumbfoundedly at them all. "They're showing me the way out..."

Maybe they are, Athena said from the ground beside me. *We should follow them.*

I stooped to pick up the bike, wincing a little as I tried to keep as much weight off my ankle as possible. I knew I couldn't ride it, but walking it along beside me seemed doable.

Slowly and steadily, Athena and I started making our way along the hiking trail. The fireflies parted as we walked toward them, blinking and encouraging us onward.

It wasn't long before a sign in the trail caught my eye. I hobbled over toward it, and surprisingly, a few fireflies floated closer, shining their lights on the wood for me.

My eyes lit up. "Athena, it's this way. We're almost home!" Relief so sweet I nearly teared up washed over me.

The fireflies continued to float along the path, and it wasn't long before there was a break in the trees, and I could see the moon reflecting off the lake.

"We made it," I said. I turned around and looked at the group of fireflies, my heart swelling. "Thank you so much. I couldn't have done it without you."

Two or three fireflies closest to me floated over and landed on my arm. They flickered their lights on and off a few times before taking off again to join their friends.

I smiled. It was like they were saying, *You're welcome.*

I started toward the lake, and in the distance, I could see Mrs. Bickford's lamppost shining in the night.

There was an SUV parked alongside the lake. I saw it as we drew closer to the water's edge. It wasn't the first time I'd seen a car here, but I wasn't sure people did a lot of fishing in the middle of the night. I didn't see any tents around, and campers were always told not to sleep so close to the cabins.

It would have been nice if the owner had been around. Maybe they could have given me a ride. Alas, the front seat was empty, and no one else was in sight.

At least, that was what I thought, until I saw a fishing boat bobbing against the shore as Athena and I walked past the SUV.

My heart filled with hope. It must have been close to dawn, and this person was already out to do some prime fishing.

I could just make out the shape of a man inside the boat, wearing fishing gear. He was perfectly still though. I wasn't surprised. Fishing was a very silent and inactive sport. At least, most of the time.

"Um, sir?" I asked, hobbling closer to the water. "I really hate to interrupt you while you're fishing, but could you possibly drive me a short ways down the road to my cabin? I was riding my bike home from work and I think I sprained my ankle."

The man didn't reply. He didn't even move.

Maybe he was hard of hearing.

I made my way closer, careful not to slip in the rain-soaked grass, and repeated my request. "Sir, I'm sorry to bother you, but would you mind giving me a ride? I think I sprained my ankle on my way home from work, and I – "

I had made it up to the side of the boat. The man's fishing rod was hanging over the edge, the bobber dangling in the water, but the line was loose.

The man, likewise, was sitting back in the boat. No, not

sitting. It was more like he was lying back, sprawled out at a strange angle.

My heart skipped as I leaned in closer. "Sir? Are you all right?"

His eyes were glassy and unfocused. His skin was so pale it was almost like paper. Bloodless. Lifeless.

With horror, my eyes fell to his neck, which was partially exposed. Right where his jugular vein would be, there were two dark holes with blue and purple bruising around them.

He was dead.

13

The tea in my hands was hot, but I hardly noticed it. The fireplace that I had been parked in front of was warm too, the logs crackling and popping. There was no cozy fox curled up in my lap, because Athena had made herself scarce once I reached the lodge, but the blanket that had been wrapped around my shoulders was well made and almost as soft as Athena's fur.

Not that any of it really mattered, not anymore.

The sun was up now, filtering in through the tall windows of the lodge, bathing the wooden floorboards in a bright light. The warm scent of cedar filled my nose as I watched Aunt Candace stare blankly at the back of the head of the man standing in front of me.

"And you didn't see anyone else around?" the man asked. He was Joe Garland, the local sheriff to Faerywood Falls. He was a tall, muscular man with a balding head, but he had kind eyes and was patient with me. His sheriff's hat lay forgotten on an end table near the fireplace.

I shook my head. "No. I hadn't seen anyone else for a long time. I was just trying to get home." I looked down at my ankle. Bliss, who'd apparently spent some time working as a nurse's assistant, had wrapped it up for me with an ice pack, trying to get some of the swelling down. By the time I'd reached the lodge, my ankle was so swollen that I could barely get my shoe off. It was now propped up on a cushy ottoman, and I had instructions not to walk on it again until I absolutely had to.

Sherriff Garland sighed and typed a few notes on his tablet. "Well, we appreciate you being willing to answer our questions," he said. "I'm sorry you had to see something so unpleasant, Miss Huffler."

I shook my head. "It's all right. I just feel so bad for the poor man."

"We will make sure that his killer is found," the sheriff said. "My boys have already taken care of the body and are investigating the area as we speak."

I knew that was supposed to give me relief, but the memory of the fisherman's dead form was still too starkly fresh in my mind.

The sheriff hesitated for a second, glancing at me.

"What is it?" I asked, shifting uncomfortably beneath his gaze.

"Just one thing..." he said, looking through his notes. "Could you describe one more time what the wounds looked like, when they were fresh? I want to make sure that I got the details right. Anything, even if it's small, could help us determine the killer."

I swallowed hard. There had been a perpetual lump in my throat since I'd told Aunt Candace and Bliss what had happened. "He was...really pale. His face was bloodless. And there was bruising on the side of his neck, and in the middle of it all, there were two black holes, like he'd been pierced or something."

"How big were the holes, exactly?" he asked.

I sighed. I'd already answered this. More than that, he could surely examine the body and see for himself. But I supposed he had to have it all on record.

"It's better if you get it all out now, dear," Aunt Candace said from behind the sheriff. "And then it will be over and you won't have to talk about it again."

I steeled my nerves. She was right. "They were...I don't know. Bigger than a needle, but narrower than a pen or a pencil? And there was no blood anywhere. If he'd been stabbed, I'm guessing it would have been everywhere." I heard myself saying the words, but it was almost as if they were coming from someone else.

Aunt Candace let out a sigh, and she looked over at Bliss, who could only shake her head. There was something to that glance that I knew they wouldn't admit in front of the sheriff, but I wanted to know what it meant.

"All right," the sheriff said, making a final note. "I just can't believe it. We've lost too many people around here lately. There is some kind of bloodthirsty animal out there. It's becoming too bold. We're going to have to deal with it." He shook his head. "Well, I've got to get this information to the station so we can start compiling suspects, even if there probably aren't any aside from some wolf or something. You take care of yourself, Miss Huffler." He turned and picked up his hat, inclining his head to Aunt Candace and Bliss. "Ladies, thank you for contacting me and letting me come and speak with her."

"Of course, Sheriff," Aunt Candace said. "We want to make sure that the killer is caught, too."

He bid us goodbye, and Mr. Terrance walked him back out to the foyer.

I let my head fall against the back of the chair, letting out a heavy exhale. I looked over at the women who had started toward me. "I'm sorry about all this."

"Oh, sweetheart, you don't have to apologize," Aunt Candace said, taking the chair beside mine. "I'm so sorry you had to go through that."

Bliss sat down cross-legged in front of the fireplace, facing me. "Are you holding up okay? Or is that still the shock talking?"

"I'm not really sure," I said. I pinched the bridge of my nose. "All I do know is that things have been super weird since I moved here. I've seen and heard the strangest things...and to be honest? A dead body is sort of at the bottom of my list."

Aunt Candace's eyes widened. "What do you mean?"

I shook my head. "You wouldn't believe me if I told you."

"Try us," Bliss said.

I met her gaze, and I saw that she really was challenging me. There was some sort of understanding there, and not for the first time, I felt a rush of affection for her and my aunt.

So I told them. I told them about the woman at the gas station, and about finding Athena. I told them how I could speak to her with my mind. I brought up Mrs. Bickford again. I explained about the book and what happened both times I'd read it. I told them about the fireflies leading me back home last night.

It was a relief to get it off my chest. I'd been stewing over it all by myself, and instead of finding answers, all I ended up with was more questions.

"So...yeah," I finally said, growing hoarse from speaking for so long. "That's what I've been dealing with lately."

Aunt Candace looked over at Bliss. "I think it's time we tell her," she said.

"Tell me what?" I asked, my heart skipping a beat.

"About the truth of Faerywood Falls," Bliss said, a sad smile climbing up her face. "The truth about you, Marianne."

I looked between her and my aunt, waiting for one of them to speak.

Finally, Aunt Candace folded her hands in front of herself and looked me dead in the eye. "Faerywood Falls is... well, it's a special and rare sort of place. It is one of the few places like it still left in the world."

"What sort of place?" I asked. "Please, just tell me. I can handle the truth."

"Yes, I think you can, too," Aunt Candace said. "There is...a magical undercurrent in Faerywood Falls. It was here long before the area was settled many years ago. It's one of the few places in the world that still has any sort of magic available in it."

It was like I had been doused in freezing cold water. And yet...it made sense. "I...had my suspicions. But that sounds crazy, you know that, right?"

Aunt Candace shrugged and glanced over at Bliss, who leaned forward.

"It definitely does. But because this is one of the few pockets of magic still existing, people who have magic in their blood, passed down from their ancestors without them even realizing it, find they are irresistibly drawn to places that still possess magic. They may never understand why, but they will just keep coming back. It feels like home to them."

I scratched my cheek absently. "I mean, I guess this place has been feeling more and more like home to me, too, but isn't it possible that these people just like this place?"

Bliss shook her head. "I get why the logical part of you

wants to make this fit into your understanding of reality, but it's just not going to, and you'll have to accept that sooner or later. Because what we are about to tell you now is going to seem even stranger."

"There's more to it than that?" I asked.

"Oh, yes, a great deal more," Aunt Candace said. "People who have magic in their blood are called the Gifted. As it sounds, these are individuals who are aware of their ability to use the magic they inherited. They have the ability to use different kinds of magic and abilities that normal humans cannot. Such folk often find the pull of magic in their veins too strong to ignore, and settle down in these places."

"So there are Gifted people living in town here?" I asked. "People who can do magic?"

Aunt Candace and Bliss both nodded. "Indeed," Aunt Candace said. "Now, most people in the town are Ungifted, and most of them are unaware of the presence of those with magical abilities. Those who are Gifted try their best to blend in with the others."

"So...who are they?" I asked. My eyes widened as I looked at them both. "Are you both Gifted?"

Bliss's face split into a grin as she looked at her mother. "Well...I am, but Mom's not," she said.

Aunt Candace nodded. "My ex-husband had magic in his blood. To be quite honest, I don't think he was aware of it at all. At least not openly."

I stared at Bliss with mingled awe and apprehension. "So what are your gifts?"

"Well, we should probably first explain how the Gifted are different from one another," she said. "We are all divided into multiple classes. This is based on our parentage and whatever magics our ancestors had. I am what is called a Spell Weaver."

"That sounds impressive," I said.

"There are others as well," Aunt Candace said. "Vampires, Shape Shifters and Beast Whisperers, Psychics and Ghost Speakers – "

I gasped. "Like Mrs. Bickford?" I asked.

They nodded.

"So she really can talk to her dead husband..." I said.

Bliss snickered at that.

"And then there are the Spell Weavers, like Bliss...and then finally, there are Faeries."

My eyes widened. "Faeries? Really?"

Bliss gave her mother a knowing look.

"What?" I asked.

"Well, it's clear that you have revealed yourself as one of the Gifted," Bliss said. "You obviously have some sort of abilities and are able to detect the magic. Speaking with your fox friend is just part of it."

Aunt Candace nodded. She leaned in closer to me. "We are not certain, but we believe that you may actually be a Faery."

The words had to sink in for a few seconds. A Faery? Me? "How...how do you know?" I asked.

"Well, the fireflies were sort of a dead give away," Bliss said. "But what really sold it was the fact that you borrowed that woman's ability at the gas station."

"How do you know?" I asked.

"Well, you didn't have the power before, and now you do," Bliss said. "It's simple, really. And you said something happened when she touched you, right? And she had those animals...most people wouldn't keep squirrels as pets, let me tell you."

"But this is where things get a little tricky," Aunt Candace said, her voice dropping. Her eyebrows knit together in a worried line. "If you are a Faery like we think you are – "

"Definitely are," Bliss interrupted.

"If you are, then you are the first Faery to appear in Faerywood Falls for a long time. It's been generations," Aunt Candace said.

Bliss nodded. "And because of it, your presence was immediately felt by the other Gifted, because there was a shifting in the balance of magic."

My eyes widened, and my heart began to beat faster. "That doesn't sound like a good thing."

"It's not a bad thing, either," Bliss said. "At least not yet. No one has identified you as *the* Faery. And that's good. Some of the Gifted in town will definitely be watching you, since you're a newcomer, and that makes everyone suspicious."

"Why would they be suspicious of me?" I asked. "And why do Faeries shift the balance of magic?"

"Because Faeries have many abilities," Aunt Candace said. "Now that you are here, they will start to awaken over time and you'll discover them. Faeries are the most powerful of the Gifted races because of this. But they also possess what might be considered the supreme ability."

"Which is what?" I asked.

"Remember how I said that you took that poor lady's ability?" Bliss said with a shrug.

"Wait...so I can steal powers?" I asked.

Bliss nodded. "Yep. Permanently. Once you have it, they don't."

I looked down at my lap, my eyes unfocused. This was all too much to take in. "It happened by accident. I don't even know how I did it."

Bliss shrugged. "That's how all of us started out. It

takes time to really understand how the magic works, because even though we have it, it's still really foreign to us."

I chewed on the inside of my lip. "Faeries in stories are known as being tricksters. Is that a real thing?"

Aunt Candace looked over at Bliss.

"We aren't really sure," Bliss said. "But a lot of myths about the Gifted are true. There are stories of some of the Faeries that lived here hundreds of years ago being manipulative or deceitful, yeah."

That was a hard blow. "But I'm not a liar. I don't want to mislead people or hurt them like that."

"That doesn't mean you will, dear," Aunt Candace said soothingly. "Unfortunately, it does mean that you might be envied or feared by the other Gifted if they were to find out your secret."

"There are some dangerous members of the other Gifted races," Bliss said. "There are good ones and bad ones in every group, but some are nastier than others."

I swallowed nervously. "So...my parents?" I asked, looking over at Aunt Candace. "My real parents, I mean?"

She sighed, shaking her head. "I'm sorry, dear, but we don't know who they were. At least one of them had to be a Faery, though, for you to have Faery in your blood."

"Does my mom know?" I asked.

Aunt Candace shook her head. "No. She doesn't know anything about your magical abilities."

"She said she found a note in the basket that she'd found me in," I said.

Aunt Candace's brow furrowed. "Yes, I know. At least I do now. She never told me when she found you."

"What did the note say?" Bliss asked.

"It said that I would be cursed if I was taken away from

Faerywood Falls," I said. "That my life would be plagued with misery and misfortune until I returned."

"Whoa," Bliss said. "And she still decided to take you anyway?"

"I guess she thought it was just nonsense or something," I said. "She didn't believe it. Neither of us did until one man I loved was murdered, and another tried to murder me."

Bliss looked away, and Aunt Candace's face fell.

"It's okay," I said. "Honestly, I've felt way better since moving back here. The nightmares I was having all the time have completely stopped, and I have more peace than I ever had before. I struggled with depression and anxiety a lot in the last few years. It's as if stepping foot into Faerywood Falls has wiped that away."

"It's the magic in your blood," Bliss said. "I was the same way."

"Well, regardless of where you came from, you are our family now," Aunt Candace said. "And we care deeply about you, Marianne. We will be here with you, and do our best to help you sort out this new part of your life."

"That's right," Bliss said. "If anyone knows what it's like going up that steep hill to learn your powers, it's me. We are going to help keep your secret, and help keep you safe."

I smiled at the two women. "Thank you...and thank you for being so honest with me. I think it's going to take some time for all of this to sink in...but as crazy as it sounds, I...I think I believe it."

"You won't have any choice but to believe it," Aunt Candace said. "The magic in you will make sure of it."

14

I spent the rest of the afternoon with Aunt Candace and Bliss. After the ordeal of a night I'd had, I didn't really want to be alone. That coupled with the revelation that I was actually some sort of supernatural creature had basically ensured I was living inside my own head, and was in no fit state to go home. I thought vaguely of Athena, but knew I didn't have to worry about her. She would have found her way back to my cabin by now and let herself in the dog door. Or maybe she would choose to stay out in the woods awhile, prowling. Either way, she would be all right.

My aunt and cousin let me sleep for a few hours that afternoon in one of the empty guest rooms. It was a sounder sleep than I'd had in years, and when I woke up, my mind was clearer and I was able to focus more. A weight that had been hanging on me for years had been slowly, ever so slowly peeling away. And my dreams that were once filled with flashes and images of my past, were normal again. Was it possible that my nightmares had something to do with the curse? Was it really gone now that I was back in Faerywood Falls?

The fireflies had been there for me, leading me. I hadn't just imagined that. The forest felt like home. Knowing it was where I'd been found seemed to bring me peace.

I smiled as I stared out the window at the place where I was really starting to feel like I belonged.

I tested my ankle and found that it didn't hurt much anymore. Sleeping with my foot up seemed to have taken away the swelling too. I wandered back downstairs and found Aunt Candace and Bliss both in the kitchen, helping prepare dinner.

I stepped up to the assembly line, choosing to chop carrots and celery for a soup stock.

"You know, I was thinking," I said as I tossed a handful of the fresh vegetables into the large copper pot in front of us. "That poor fisherman...now that you told me everything that you did about the townspeople, it made me see the situation in a whole new light. What if those weren't stab wounds in his neck at all, but bitemarks?"

Aunt Candace glanced over at me. "I would have thought you would want to think about anything else besides that poor man," she said.

"I know," I said. "But I guess I sort of experienced this in my life once already, when Jacob, the first man I ever loved, was murdered. It was a horrible time in my life, and it wasn't until the killer was found that I felt Jacob had any justice. Even then, it was still hard to swallow. But with how many people in this town are not Gifted, or don't know about the Gifted, then the chances of finding the real killer are a lot less, aren't they?"

Aunt Candace gave me a considering look. "Yes, I suppose that is true. And the bigger problem is that magic can be very deceiving, and that could make it even harder to distinguish the real killer."

I tossed some celery into the pot. "The first thought that popped into my mind was that it must have been a vampire, right?" I said, my eyebrows raising. I couldn't believe I was talking about a vampire as if it were a real thing. I couldn't be sure part of that wasn't because the shock hadn't completely worn off yet. "The marks were close enough together that it could have been made from fangs. Do vampires have fangs?" I asked.

Bliss nodded. "They almost pop out of their mouths when they're ready to drink. It's really creepy."

Aunt Candace gave Bliss a look that I recognized.

I said, "Look, Aunt Candace, I know you're trying to protect me, but you don't have to – "

"You've been through enough," she said. "What you need now is rest and relaxation, not to get yourself involved in that poor man's murder."

"I think she has some sort of right," Bliss said from the other side of her mother. She was busy chopping up some fresh rosemary from their garden. "I mean, she was the one who found him after all. Maybe helping figure out whodunnit will help her have some closure."

Aunt Candace sighed. "Well...I can't say that I'm not at least a little curious," she said. She then turned back to me. "Do you remember that castle up on the mountain that we saw from the front of Abe's shop?" she asked.

I nodded.

"That's Blackburn castle," she said. "And like I said, old family. They've lived here a long time."

"They're the vampires?" I asked, the color draining from my cheeks. It was one thing to hear about these mythical creatures existing, and it was another thing entirely to actually be pointed in their direction.

Bliss nodded. "Yes. Cain Blackburn is a nice guy. I've met him a few times – "

"You've done what?" her mother asked, rounding on Bliss, her dark eyebrows a hard, thin line.

Bliss grinned apologetically. "Easy, Mom. I just met him at that Spell Weaver event we had last summer. Apparently he and the head weaver had some sort of business dealing."

"That does seem like a more likely alliance than vampires and, say, werewolves," I said. "Do they hate each other?"

"The vampires really don't like anyone," Bliss said. "It was a business deal of convenience, nothing more." She glanced over at the clock. "Well, we could always go talk to Cain. See what he might know about it. It'll have to be a few hours from now, though. They don't do well with sunlight, you know."

"At least I know that already," I said. I massaged my temples. "It feels like I've put too much info into my brain too fast."

"You'll get used to it," Bliss said.

It took some time, but we eventually convinced Aunt Candace to let us go. Bliss insisted on going with me to protect me, being a spell weaver and all. My aunt kept telling us that we had no reason to go over there and ask the Blackburns what they had to do with the murder, but Bliss insisted that we did, since I was the one who'd witnessed the murder and realized it must have had some sort of Gifted cause, that we were just informally helping the sheriff get to the bottom of it. We weren't sure if anyone would buy that, but it was the truth, and it was better than lying about it in the first place. I shot that idea down in the very beginning.

Bliss drove us up to the castle when it got dark, and I couldn't sit still. My heart was in my throat as we made our way through the thick tree-lined roads, the moon shining high overhead.

"Looks like it's almost full..." Bliss commented, shaking her head.

"Is that bad?" I asked.

"Definitely," she said. "It's when the shape shifters change without control. They all have their means of dealing with it, but it always seems like us spell weavers are the ones who have to keep the illusion going."

"What about these vampires?" I asked. "What can you tell me about them?"

Bliss sighed as she stared out the windshield. "Well... there's not really a whole lot to say. They've been living here for a long time. It's the same people who built the castle a few centuries ago. Because vampires are immortal and everything. They can die by violence but not natural causes."

I swallowed hard. That was probably going to take me awhile to acknowledge. Or even believe.

"So are they actually a family?" I asked.

"No," Bliss said, furrowing her brow, and shaking her head. "They say they are so the people who are not Gifted in town don't think it's strange when a man they met when they were twenty looks the exact same when they meet him at eighty. Anyway, only two of them are actually related."

"I can't imagine vampires living in a town of ordinary humans without something going horribly wrong," I said. That further solidified my theory about the vampires being the killers. Especially in light of the bat-like silhouette I had seen in the forest the other night.

Bliss shook her head. "It's not like that, honestly. They keep to themselves entirely. No one in town likes Cain – he's the town mortician, but he's also the vampire faction's leader. People also don't come up here much because there's rumors that the castle is haunted."

"Really?" I asked.

"Yeah. Stories make their way through the town about some sort of female apparition that screams late in the night," Bliss said.

"Is that true?" I asked.

"It is real, but she's not a ghost," Bliss said. "It's Cain's sister, and he keeps her locked up because when she is crazed with bloodlust, she's a danger to the community."

"Wow," I said. "I'm leaning more and more on the theory it was a vampire who killed that poor fisherman."

We rounded a corner and the castle came into view. This close, it definitely had the same shape as a castle, but on a smaller scale. It looked like it was meant to be a replica of a medieval structure. It wasn't without its modern amenities, though. I could see the gate was all high tech as we pulled up.

Bliss rolled down the window and leaned out to a speaker beside a keypad and fingerprint scanner. Did that sort of technology work on vampire flesh?

"Blackburn estate, to whom am I speaking?"

Bliss gave me a sidelong look – *what's with the formality?*

"Bliss Brooks," she said. "We're here to speak with someone about the recent murder of a fisherman down by Faerywood Falls lake."

There was silence for a moment. "Mr. Blackburn has approved your request. Please proceed to the house, do not stray from the main drive, and walk only to the front door. Am I understood?"

"Yeah, sure," Bliss said, putting the car back in drive.

The tall metal gate in front of us slid open and Bliss drove slowly through.

The driveway meandered up the mountainside. We passed gardens and pools. A set of tennis courts had been carved into the hillside, and I thought I could see a full size Olympic pool with a view of the whole valley below.

"These people really live in luxury, don't they?" I asked, finding myself looking at a small golf course, the sand traps reflecting the glow of the moon.

"When you live for hundreds of years, money doesn't matter anymore," Bliss said. "You can basically make endless amounts of it."

We parked the car beside a few others, all of which probably cost more than all four years of my college tuition. We stepped outside into the cool night air and stared up at the house. Most of the lights were on inside, pools of warmth flooding out onto the ground outside.

A silhouette of a petite woman stepped in front of one of the windows, paused there for a moment, and then continued on past.

We started up the wide, stone stairs, and I worried that my knees were going to give out on me. I was going to meet a vampire, face to face. Maybe I already had in my life, but never realized it. "I'm really glad you're with me," I said to Bliss, my heartbeat hammering inside my ears. "I couldn't do this without knowing that you can protect us."

"Yeah, about that..." Bliss said under her breath.

I wheeled around and looked back at her. She was a few steps lower than I was, her hand holding the marble railing with a white-knuckled grip as she ascended. She gave me a sheepish look. "I'm really only an apprentice. I mean, I know some pretty cool stuff, but to keep vampires away..."

"So you lied to me?" I asked.

"Not lied," Bliss said. "Just...maybe stretched the truth a bit?"

I let out a shaky breath. It was pointless to get angry with her when it seemed she was just as scared as I was.

We reached the enormous wooden front doors, easily two stories tall. We looked at one another. I noticed her face was as pale as mine felt.

I lifted a fist to knock on the door, but it began to swing inward at the motion.

It didn't open very far before a tall, slender man slipped outside. He was wearing a dark suit with tails as if he were in the middle of some big, fancy party. His shoes shone in the lamplight on the front deck. When he turned around, my stomach dropped.

Whatever image I'd concocted in my head for a vampire, this man was not it. I'd imagined pale skin, black, pupil-less eyes, pointed teeth. But the man standing in front of me was the classic tall, dark, and handsome. His hair was slicked back elegantly, as if it was effortless. He had high cheekbones, a wide jaw, and deep set eyes that were so green I wondered if they were contacts.

He was one of the most attractive men I'd ever seen in my life. It was as if he'd stepped out of a magazine or a movie or something.

"Good evening, ladies..." he said with a sweeping bow. He grinned at us as he righted himself, making my heart flutter. "What brings you to my humble home?"

I glanced upward at his "humble" home, and wondered if in comparison to all his other vampire friends, it was small. "Hi, Mr. Blackburn," I said nervously. "Should I call you Mr. Blackburn?" I asked.

His smile widened. "Please, call me Cain. And what may I call you beautiful women?"

My cheeks turned pink. "Oh...um, I'm Marianne, and this is my cousin Bliss."

Bliss lifted her hand in a small wave of hello.

There was a flash of recognition in his eyes. "You're a spell weaver, aren't you?" he asked Bliss.

"Yes," she said.

"I thought I recognized you," he said, and a knowing smile crept up his face. "Very well. What may I do for you?"

It was hard to form words in my mind as he turned his bright green eyes on me. I couldn't remember the last time that a man had been so attractive to me that he'd numbed my brain. I was tongue tied.

"We are looking into the death of the fisherman down by the lake," Bliss said, thankfully stepping in for me. "It happened the other night."

"Ah, yes," Cain said, shaking his head, concern furrowing his brow. "How unfortunate for the poor man."

"We think he was murdered," Bliss said.

Cain gave her a steady look in return for her hardened one. "I imagine I am a suspect then?" he asked. "Or one of my kin?"

Bliss and I looked at one another.

"Well, it only makes sense," he said. "Why would you come up here otherwise? Yes, I know the story about what happened. I saw the body shortly afterward."

I blinked at him.

"I'm the town's mortician," he said kindly and with a smile as if he'd just told me that he was a veterinarian or a dentist.

"Right," I said. I didn't ask why a man of his obvious wealth would choose such an occupation. As a vampire, perhaps the job gave him access to things I didn't want to think about.

"Well, I will tell you both right now that I was not involved in the poor man's death in any way," he said, folding his arms over his chest. "But how are you two involved?"

Bliss gave me an anxious shake of the head, but I looked away.

"I was the one who found the victim," I said. "I was on my way home from work, got lost in the woods, and found him near my cabin."

Cain's eyes narrowed slightly, as if they were lenses focusing more intently on me. "I see. Well, you'll soon find, Miss Marianne, that it does not do to linger in the forest so late at night."

His words sent a chill down my spine, but his voice was so deep and so smooth that I just wanted him to keep talking.

"How can we believe that you aren't the one who did it?" Bliss asked, folding her arms.

Cain returned her gaze easily. "Because the marks on the neck of the corpse were clearly an attempt to pin the killing on my family and me," he said. "And a poor one, at that. My kin are not murderers."

"What about your sister?" Bliss asked.

"My sister has been restrained for the safety of everyone in Faerywood Falls," Cain said. "She has not stepped foot out of this house in a very long time. I assure you, it was not us."

I looked over at Bliss helplessly. He could have been lying, but how could we know for sure?

"I have security cameras covering every inch of my property," Cain said, his voice darkening and his gaze hardening. "If you would like, I could provide you with the evidence."

"That won't be necessary," Bliss said with a nervous smile. She looked at me. "Well, thank you, Cain, I think that was everything. Thank you very much for your time."

His charm returned, and he looked over at me. "Well, thank you for stopping by. It has been a long time since I've met anyone quite so...charming. And with such lovely eyes..."

Bliss reached over and grabbed my arm, pulling me toward her. "Thanks again, Cain. See you around."

"Indeed you will," he said, his eyes following after us as we descended the steps. "I look forward to it."

15

On the way back, Bliss didn't say anything. Her hands gripped the steering wheel, her face completely void of color as she stared wide-eyed out the windshield. Her lips were turning bright pink as she continued to gnaw on them.

"Well, that was interesting," I said.

"Yeah, you're telling me," Bliss said as we pulled out onto the road, the high tech gate sliding closed behind us. She turned and looked at me, her green eyes huge. "Weren't you freaking out up there?"

"Um...kind of, I guess," I said. "I thought he was nice enough, considering he didn't have to talk to us at all."

She suppressed a shiver. "It looked like he was going to eat you or something. I was starting to worry about how I was going to get you out of there."

"I don't think he'd do that," I said.

"How would you know?" she asked.

I shrugged. "I don't."

Her eyes narrowed. "You thought he was cute, didn't you?"

I blushed. "No, I did not."

"You do realize that vampires are, by nature, really good looking to humans to basically draw them in so they can more easily hunt and kill them, right?" she asked.

Another chill ran down my spine, making goosebumps appear on my legs. "All right, then you must have thought he was good looking, too."

"I was too busy reminding myself of the fact that I could have been a vampire's third course tonight if I wasn't careful," Bliss said.

"Well, regardless, we're still at square one," I said with a heavy sigh. "We aren't any closer to finding out who actually did it. There's no way to know whether it was one of the vampires or if Cain was telling the truth when he said whoever is guilty was trying to pin it on his kin."

"That does make sense, in a way," Bliss said. "The factions all despise each other, so of course they'd try to blame someone else. One thing we can be sure of, though. Cain wouldn't have offered to show us his security footage unless he was sure it wouldn't incriminate any of his own. Whether that's because he doctored the footage or because there's just nothing to see I don't know."

I groaned. "Is it possible we're barking up the wrong tree altogether?" I asked.

"What do you mean?" Bliss asked.

"What if this is nothing more than some kind of animal after all?" I asked. "Weren't you and your mom talking recently about some hunters who had been killed in the forest? What if it's just like a rabid animal? A wolf or a bear or something?"

"I don't know," Bliss said. "That's what all the non-Gifted people in town seem to think, but Mom and I have never been convinced of that. And neither was Cain, either, at least in this case. If he thought it was just an animal, I think he would have said as much."

"You're probably right," I said. "So, then who else could have done it? Made this look like an animal attack?"

"Well, I mean, the shape shifters literally transform into animals," Bliss said. "It is possible that the poor fisherman was bit while one of them was in their animal state."

"Werewolves," I said.

"Among other things, yes," Bliss said. "The leader of their faction is a man named Dr. Lucan Valerio, and he – "

"Wait," I said, my heart skipping a beat. "Is he this really good looking man with reddish hair and a beard? Really tall? Really well dressed? Italian?"

"Yeah," Bliss said. "How'd you know?"

"Your mom and I met him outside of Abe's antique store," I said. "He's the owner of the bank in town?"

"And of the small historical center and museum," Bliss said with a nod. "And you thought he was attractive, too?"

I shrugged. "He was, what's wrong with that?"

"You've now admitted that two of the most powerful men in Faerywood Falls were attractive," she said.

I gave her a small smile. "You should be surprised. It's been awhile since I was attracted to anyone. It sort of makes you less inclined to want to date when your fiancé tries to poison you..." I pushed those old fears away. "So, that guy I met turns into a werewolf, huh?"

"Yeah," Bliss said. "I haven't seen it, but one of the other spell weavers I know said she saw it happen once. He's apparently a silver wolf with gold eyes."

My heart skipped, and my jaw fell open. "I've seen him, too..."

"What?" Bliss asked, shooting anxious glances at me

while still trying to keep her eyes on the dark, winding road. "When? Where?"

"On the way to meet you and your mom for the first time," I said. "I almost hit a wolf that looked just like that."

We were quiet for a moment. I was remembering the golden eyes that had watched me out of the trees the night I found Athena. Had that been Dr. Valerio too? It seemed likely.

"You guys did say that they would all be watching me, didn't you?" I asked.

"Yeah, we did..." Bliss said.

I chewed on the inside of my cheek. "Well, we aren't going to get any answers driving around like this. We should go see Dr. Valerio."

"No," Bliss said, maybe too quickly.

I looked over at her. "Why not?"

"Look, it's the middle of the night. I'm sure you're exhausted. I sure as anything am. I'm still creeped out about the vampires, and honestly, it's almost the full moon and those shape shifters are not exactly going to be in a state of mind where they're able to communicate."

"Oh," I said.

"It would really be better if we just went tomorrow when you get off work," Bliss said with a heavy sigh. "Besides, Dr. Valerio is probably having one of his swanky soirees tonight, and we would want to be around all those shape shifters like we'd want a hole in the head."

"Got it," I said. "We'll just go tomorrow, then."

I really was tired. I'd slept a little that afternoon, but it wasn't enough. The events of the last day were still rolling around in my head, and it was probably best if I just gave myself some time to process it all.

I said goodbye to Bliss and Aunt Candace when we got

back to the lodge, and made my way back to the cabin in the dark. I kept my eyes on the surrounding forest as I drove, hoping not to run into any more pairs of yellow eyes staring out at me in the darkness. I hoped Bliss was right about Dr. Valerio having a party that night so I wouldn't have to worry about seeing him.

It was strange to think that the man I'd met that night was a vampire, and the man I'd met outside Abe's place was a shape shifter. But then, Bliss was a spell weaver, so it wasn't all that weird, I guessed.

Maybe I still hadn't come to terms with her or her powers yet, either.

When I arrived at the cabin, I walked inside and found Athena curled up on the foot of my bed. She lifted her head when I walked inside.

I was worried about you, she said. *Why did you take so long to come home?*

I told her about my conversation with Sheriff Garland, the visit to the Blackburn castle, and my intention to visit Dr. Valerio the next day.

I lay down on the bed, yawning as Athena seemed to settle down. *I'm glad you're home.*

"Yeah, me too," I said.

For as crazy as my day had been, I was elated to slide between my covers and lay my head down on the pillow.

Vampires. Shape shifters. Faeries.

As weird as it all sounded, to me, it made sense. As if I had waited my whole life to hear that there was something more to this world than the day in and day out existence I'd been living. Everything had been pointing me to this.

I wasn't alone anymore.

16

Ma...rianne...

I squeezed my eyes shut tight. There were fireflies all around, dancing above my head, swaying back and forth in the evening breeze. A mesmerizing melody played somewhere far away, and I was content. Completely content.

Ma...rianne...

No. The nightmares were gone. The curse had been broken. I was free.

Marianne!

I opened my eyes, my heart racing.

Athena was standing on my chest, her little black nose almost touching mine. *Marianne, your tiny talking box is making sounds.*

She was right. My cell phone was ringing away on the dining table in the kitchen.

I rubbed at my eyes as Athena climbed down off me. The sky outside the windows was pink as dawn was coming. I dragged myself out of the comfort and sanctuary of my bed to pull myself over to the phone.

"Hello?" I answered.

"Marianne, hello, it's Abe," said the voice on the other end.

I sank down into the chair beside the table, rubbing at my eyes. "Oh, good morning, Mr. Cromwell."

"I'm sorry to call so early, but there's a bit of a problem," Abe said.

My heart skipped a beat. "A problem? What sort of problem?" I asked.

The old man sighed on the other end of the phone. "Well, there's been a robbery at the store," he said, his voice heavy. I wondered if he'd slept at all the night before.

"A robbery?" I asked. "When did this happen?"

"It was after you locked up on Saturday," Mr. Cromwell said.

My stomach was twisting into knots, and my brain was waking up quickly. "Was there a lot of damage?"

"No, actually, that's the strange part," he said. "The person must have gotten in through the door some way, and then locked everything back up before they left to avoid suspicion. They somehow got in here without me ever hearing it."

"Was anything stolen?" I asked.

"Yes, several things," Mr. Cromwell said heavily. "A few mirrors, some glass jars, a very expensive jade statuette, and a red leather-bound book."

My stomach did another summersault. "Was it that strange book with all the letters inside?" I asked.

"Yes, how'd you know?" he asked.

My cheeks colored. "I've been looking at that book, trying to figure out what it was, exactly."

"Yes, I tried to do the same many times," he said. "I gave

up eventually. I think it's nothing more than a glorified word finding game."

I wondered if he was able to see the glowing and shifting words. Something told me that wasn't the case.

Suddenly, it was as if I was struck in the face. I sat up straight, staring around my tiny cabin, my heart racing. I hadn't been the only one who had been interested in that book... "Mr. Cromwell, do you know who broke into the shop?" I asked.

"No idea," he said. "I've had the police here already this morning. Seems they've got their hands full with a potential murder case. Faerywood Falls is keeping those boys busy right now."

"Um..." I said, and decided against telling him that I'd been the one to find the murder victim's body. The poor man had enough to deal with. "Well, I don't want to be presumptuous, but I think I may have some idea of a person who might have gone to great lengths to get their hands on that book that was stolen," I said.

"Go on," Abe said quietly.

My knee was bouncing as I tried to find the best words. "Well, there was this woman who came into the shop on Saturday, not long before I closed up for the day. She'd found that book on a table that I'd set it down on. Honestly, I'd been meaning to ask you if I could just buy the book from you for a while, and I'd forgotten to set it aside. Well, when she asked if she could purchase it, I told her it wasn't for sale, and she became very angry with me, telling me that you would regret ever not selling her something."

Mr. Cromwell sighed. "Oh, I'm not mad at you, Marianne. If you wanted that book, then I have no problem with you telling her it wasn't for sale. But, do you by any chance remember what this woman looked like?"

"Yeah," I said. "She was shorter than I was, with blonde hair with blue ends, and purple eyes. And she was wearing these brightly colored striped stockings – "

"That's Silvia Griffin," Mr. Cromwell said with another heavy sigh. "Oh, boy..."

"What?" I asked. "Did I do something wrong?"

"No," Mr. Cromwell said. "But if this is Silvia's doing..."

"Well, if we suspect her, couldn't we just call the police and tell them what happened that day?" I asked.

"No, unfortunately we couldn't," Mr. Cromwell said. "She works on the city council and has a great deal of influence. If I were to challenge her about anything, she wouldn't hesitate to close my shop up for good."

"How terrible," I said.

He sighed. "Well...I don't know how she did it, or even if she did it. We have no proof either way. Maybe Marie was right...we should have gotten those security cameras installed a few years ago."

My heart saddened at the sorrow in his voice when he spoke about his late wife. "I'm sorry, Mr. Cromwell. What can I do?"

"Not much, I guess," he said. "Would you be willing to come in today still? Help me do inventory, make sure nothing else was taken?"

"Of course," I said. "Just give me a little while to shower and I'll be right over."

"Take your time," he said with an attempt at his usual enthusiasm. "I'll be here."

I hung up the phone, and anger seeped into my bones. That awful woman who'd stormed out of the shop the other day...she had to be the one responsible. But how? We couldn't prove it, but that had to be it. It had to be her.

And she had the book. That book was dangerous. I

didn't know if she was aware of its power or not, but that didn't matter. If she messed around with the book like I did and she had any sort of Gifted abilities, who knew what might happen?

Worse yet, what if she knew what the book was when she saw it, and that was why she was so angry about it?

I showered and ate something quickly for breakfast, Athena keeping her beady black eyes on me the whole time.

You're quite restless, she said.

"Yeah, I am," I said, shrugging on my jacket, and untucking my hair from inside of the collar. "I have a bad feeling about all this."

Athena's ears twitched. *Yes, I do too, I must admit. I'm coming with you today.*

I didn't have the heart to say no. In a way, I was happy to know she was going to be there with me.

We decided to take my car to the shop this time. After my little accident in the woods, I didn't feel up to riding the bike. The muscles were still slightly sore in my ankle, although thankfully I hadn't done too much damage.

Mr. Cromwell seemed all right when I got to the shop, but I noticed that he disappeared rather quickly after I unlocked the front door. I didn't think he wanted to answer any questions from patrons that might come in. I didn't really blame him.

What I hadn't accounted for was the fact that all the customers walking through the door directed their questions, many of which were incredibly invasive into Mr. Cromwell's privacy, at me. It wasn't even noon before I was almost ready to lock up and join him upstairs.

I was sweeping near the back counter, trying to keep my head down and look busy so nosy customers wouldn't bother me when someone approached me. "Um, I'm sorry, but do you work here?"

I rolled my eyes and looked up at the man. He was maybe ten years younger than Mr. Cromwell, with thick, greying hair that he kept cleanly trimmed. He had bright blue eyes that were heavy with sadness, and it sapped all the frustration from me. "Oh...yes, I do. How can I help you?" I asked, leaning the broom against the counter.

"My name is Lenny, and I own the diner next door. Abe and I have been friends for a long time. I wanted to see how he was doing after the break in," he said.

"It seems like everyone in town knew about it before I did," I said.

"Don't feel too bad," Lenny said with a small smile. "News always travels quickly in small towns like this. And you must be Marianne?" he asked, holding his hand out to me.

I smiled and shook it. "Yes, I am."

"I'm sorry I'm so late in introducing myself. I was out of town when you moved into the area. I'd meant to come over and introduce myself on Saturday, but that's our busiest day, and I couldn't find the chance to get away," he said.

"That's all right," I said, walking back around behind the counter. My eyes darted to a group of old women who had stepped inside. Hopefully they weren't another party of town gossips. "And to answer your earlier question, Mr. Cromwell is doing all right, just a bit shaken I guess. There were some valuable things taken, and it's unsettling that the robber didn't leave any evidence behind."

Lenny slid his hands into the pockets of his trousers and shook his head with a sigh. "That's really too bad. It was very strange, because the night it happened, I was chatting with one of our regulars while he was eating his dinner. Out of the window, we saw some suspicious movement over here. We knew it couldn't have been Abe, he never drives himself, and there's no way anyone would come at night unless it was an emergency. Well, the gentleman that I was talking with was a security guard for many years, and so he offered to go and investigate. I was nervous as I stood at the window and watched. The gentleman, Burt Cassidy was his name, walked around the whole building, and a few minutes later, he hurried over and told me that he thought someone may have broken in. He told me he was going to call the police, and then he left. Sure enough, the police showed up a short while later, but they didn't find anything that suggested there had been a break in."

"How strange," I said.

Lenny nodded, and I saw a tightness in his eyes. "Yes... it's terrible enough that poor Abe had this happen to him, but worse than that, Burt was found dead the next morning."

My stomach lurched. *Calm down, Marianne. It's not impossible that there would be two dead bodies found the same day that you found the fisherman.*

"That's awful," I said.

Lenny wiped at his eyes with his fingers. "Yeah, I guess after he'd spoken with the police, he'd set out to do some fishing. It was his favorite thing to do since he'd retired just a few years ago. He and his wife moved back to the area; she grew up here. I saw Liza yesterday... It broke my heart."

My own heart was beating quickly in my ears. "What happened?"

"Well, they don't really know," Lenny said, folding his arms across his chest. "They found him in his fishing boat. The police are saying that it looks like something attacked him, just like those hunters that have turned up dead lately."

He sighed heavily, and looked like he was carrying the weight of the world on his shoulders. "It's just terrible, so many deaths. I know all of us are getting real tired of going to these funerals and having to watch the families suffer."

So it wasn't a coincidence after all. That man was the same one I had found in the fishing boat down on the lake. Lenny was the last person to see him alive. This Burt Cassidy was the one who had noticed the break in...and then he turned up dead right after...

"Lenny, do you mind if I ask you a question?" I asked, my blood turning cold. "Burt was the person who reported the break in, right?"

Lenny nodded. "Yeah. He claimed he saw someone moving around inside, and it wasn't Abe."

I sighed.

"If it's all right, I'm just going to sneak up the back stairs and go see Abe," Lenny said, moving to step around me.

"Sure, no problem," I mumbled, but my mind was elsewhere.

I was figuring out who had killed Burt Cassidy.

17

"Bliss? Hey, it's me," I said, snapping my seat belt into place, my fingers trembling.

"Hey, what's up, Marianne?" Bliss asked. "Out of work already?"

"No," I said, glancing over my shoulder as I backed my SUV up out of its spot. "I'm leaving early."

Athena was sitting in the front seat like a cat, all curled up with her tail wrapped around her, but one eye was opened wide and staring at me.

"Why?" Bliss asked.

"Do you know who Silvia Griffin is?" I asked, and with every fiber of my being, I hoped that she would say no.

"Yeah, why?" she asked.

My stomach sank. "She's not a spell weaver, is she?" I asked, the last of my hope hinging on her answer.

"Yeah, she's one of the seats on the council of eleven – our sort of leadership board – and has been for a long, long time. Why?" Bliss asked.

"Is she...a nice person?" I asked, hoping still yet again for another out.

"Oh, no way," Bliss said, her tone totally changing. "She's the definition of what a cliché spell weaver is. She's nasty, selfish, uses any opportunity to toe the line of what the council of eleven has agreed on as right and wrong...she even wears these hideous striped stockings. She probably has a million pairs, all different colors."

"Oh, boy..." I said.

"What is it?" Bliss asked.

"I think..." I couldn't believe I was about to say this out loud. "I think she killed the fisherman, who I found out today was named Burt Cassidy."

"What?" Bliss asked.

"Someone broke into the antiques store, and I think it was her, because she came into the shop on Saturday and tried to buy that magic book from me. When I wouldn't give it to her, she threatened me and stormed out. Then that book along with some other items that are probably magical in some way turned up missing after a strange break in. The weirdest part is that the man who reported the break in is the one who ended up dead." I said.

"You think she killed him to keep her secret?" Bliss asked.

"I know it's a long shot, but it's the only lead we have. And that book is dangerous, Bliss. We have to get it back from her, and I think I'm the only one who knows what it really is."

I heard Bliss click her tongue in annoyance. "This is so like Silvia to do something as terrible as that."

"We have to find her," I said. "Do you have any idea how I might locate her?"

"Oh, definitely," Bliss said. "We spell weavers have ways of finding one another. Meet me here at the lodge. I'll get the rest of the council on the phone and hopefully by the time you get here, they'll have called back to say they've found her."

FIND HER THEY DID. It turned out that Bliss was right. The members of the council of eleven evidently knew some handy spells that were able to locate Silvia Griffin – and they were shocked enough at her behavior that they were willing to use their knowledge to help us.

"She's tried to conceal herself," Bliss informed me when I arrived at the lodge just as she got off the phone with a council member. "And she almost succeeded, too, if she'd only remembered that it is much easier to locate her when we have a piece of her hair."

"How did the other spell weavers get that?" I asked.

Bliss shrugged. "Simple. They went to her house and found it on her pillow."

Magic really was strange, but I wanted to find Silvia, so I just went with it.

"She's somewhere up on a mountain trail," Bliss said. "There aren't any houses or cabins or anything there. She's probably using a weaver hut or something."

"Weaver hut?" I asked.

"Transportable spell weaver accommodations," Bliss said nonchalantly. "Also easy to hide from non-Gifted people."

"So she's in hiding…" I said.

Bliss nodded. "The council tried to contact her, and she severed communication. She might not be up there all that much longer."

"Then we need to catch her," I said, my brow furrowing. "She needs to pay for what she's done."

"I agree, but are you sure you really want to be the one to confront her?" Bliss asked.

"Yes," I said. "Because if I'm a faery like you say, maybe there's something I can do to stop her. At least, I'll have more chance than anyone who's not Gifted. Best to leave the police out of this until we know exactly what we're up against."

"I can't go along and help you," Bliss said apologetically. "The council have forbidden me as an apprentice to involve myself in a fight with a spell weaver as powerful as Silvia. I've taken oaths and I'm bound to obey them."

"I understand," I said.

"I don't think the council will help you further in this either," she said. "They're too busy debating with one another how best to handle the matter internally without spilling our secrets to the Ungifted. It could take them ages to reach a decision."

"Time we don't have," I said. "Silvia could be planning anything right now. I've got to get at her before she's had a chance to prepare."

Bliss agreed. She gave me the directions and sent me on my way before Aunt Candace figured out what we were up to. My aunt would never have let me leave if she knew what was happening.

I followed my GPS up the long, winding roads to the mountains overlooking the lake, my heart in my throat the whole time. What was going to happen when I got up there? What was I going to do? Or say? I didn't have any knowledge of these powers I supposedly possessed as a faery. Maybe I could reveal what I was to Silvia, and that would be enough to make her back down.

But what if she turned around and told everyone my secret? No...that wasn't going to work.

The mountaintop came into sight, and my heart was pumping so fast I was certain it was going to beat right out of my chest. The road was definitely more like a hiking trail. My SUV barely made it through some of the narrow walk-ways, and it wasn't until I found a walking bridge over a gorge that I knew I had to make it the rest of the way on foot.

I was hoping against all hope that she was still going to be there when I reached the summit. Sweat trickled down my back as I walked up the steep, rocky trails, the shoes I'd thrown on that morning less than suitable for hiking.

Athena, who'd come with me, hurried along beside me, her nose pointed in the air for any hint of Silvia's scent. Her coat gleamed in the sun, but I didn't have time to appreciate her or any of the other beauty around us.

The sun beat down on me, and it wasn't long before the back of my neck started to feel raw and swollen. I kept wiping sweat out of my eyes, and my breath was coming in sharp pants.

Almost there. I could make it. I had to make it. Some-thing deep down told me that bad things were going to happen if I didn't reach Silvia.

The wind rushing through the trees picked up, pushing against my back as if to urge me onwards. The branches clapped against one another, almost as if in applause.

It was like a light glowing within me, dim at first. I reached out toward it with my very soul. It was like a sweet voice, calling me back home.

Keep...going...

I felt like the leaves were singing to me.

It's as if the forest is awakening at your presence... Athena said, her eyes shifting from tree to tree.

Courage flooded through me as I continued to climb.

We reached the summit, and the line of trees gave way

to a wide expanse of sky and valley below, visible over a cliff face. It stretched across the horizon like a scroll being unrolled, in all manner of greens and blues and grays. The lake that I saw out of my windows every morning, and gazed at every night as Athena and I enjoyed dinner together, was like a disc of glass far below, perfectly flat, reflecting the puffy white clouds in the brilliantly blue sky above.

A pair of hawks flew overhead, screeching to each other.

The hilltop was deserted as I looked around, the wind whipping my face, tossing my hair against my eyelashes. It was a good thing that I wasn't afraid of heights. The path was narrow up here, and as I stared down the cliff, I could see the sheer drop back down the side of the mountain, even from where I stood.

I took a shuddering glance. I was safe as long as I didn't move too close to the edge.

I glanced at the GPS on my phone again. This was where Bliss had directed me. I also remembered that Bliss had said Silvia had been trying to hide from the spell weaver's council.

I balled my hands into fists, anger fueling my courage. "Silvia!" I shouted, staring around. "I know you're here. Show yourself."

Nothing happened for a moment, but just as quickly as I had blinked, a woman was standing there a short distance away, her violet eyes flashing dangerously. She was twirling some of her blue dyed hair around the end of her finger, smirking at me.

"Well, well," she said, taking a few slow, exaggerated steps toward me. "If it isn't the little shopkeeper. What brings you here?"

A ripple of fear passed over the pond of relative calmness I was trying to hold onto. "I know that you broke into Mr. Cromwell's store on Saturday night."

She shrugged her shoulders. "Yeah? So what?"

"So what?" I asked, indignant. "You're kidding, right? That's a crime."

"It was a crime for him to keep this book all hidden away like he was," she said, snapping her fingers. The book appeared in a puff of purple smoke and landed in her outstretched hand. "Or rather, it was you who was to blame, I guess. You're the one who refused to sell it to me in the first place."

"Because it's mine," I said.

She looked up at me, tilting her head to the side. She let out a shrill laugh. "My, my. Have some propensity for magic yourself, huh? What are you, a spell weaver? A beast talker?" Her eyes fell on Athena, who was standing loyally at my side. "No wonder you wanted it. But too bad, so sad. I have it now. Finders keepers, and all that..."

She snapped her fingers, and the book disappeared again.

"It wasn't just the book," I said. "You also killed Burt Cassidy because he was the one who reported the robbery in the first place."

A malicious smile spread across Silvia's pretty face. "Yes, I did. My, aren't you just the little detective? The sheriff should hire you; he might actually get something done for once." She let out a sharp laugh at her own joke. Then her face darkened. "That fool Burt Cassidy saw me leave, and after calling the police, he tailed me for a while. I was able to lose him, but I knew he was onto me. For all I knew, he only held back my identity from the police in hopes of blackmailing me later. So, I followed him and killed him to make sure he didn't talk." She kicked at a rock with the tip of her heeled boot. "It was easy, really. I just used a handy spell from that book to freeze his heart."

I remembered how I had stumbled across a freezing spell inside the book myself, when I'd accidentally broken the clock in the shop. Possibly it was the same spell Silvia had used, although she had obviously known better than me how to target the spell in the direction she wanted.

She continued, "Then, as he was dying, all it took was using a sharp object to puncture his neck to look like teeth marks. Couldn't have the police suspecting some*one* instead of some *creature*, right? Especially with all those hunters getting killed recently. Not that I had anything to do with their deaths, mind you. Small loss, though, I'm sure."

I gaped at her, my blood running cold. "You talk about murdering a man like it was no more trouble than taking out the trash."

"Yes, well, I didn't do it just for myself, you know. We spell weavers have to do anything and everything we can to ensure that the secret of our existence is never discovered by the Ungifted," Silvia said, examining her black fingernails.

I could only stare at her. She'd admitted she'd done it without batting an eye. Bliss had said that she was less than pleasant, but to be so open to murder...there was something truly wrong with this woman.

"Oh, yes, I know that I'll catch it from the council of eleven for killing him, but they'll come around when they see what a threat he posed to us overall," Silvia said, pacing back and forth across the walking path. My eyes followed her as she walked right up to the edge of the cliff and stared down into the gorge's depths.

"He wouldn't have posed a threat at all if you hadn't gone in and stolen that book," I said.

"And I wouldn't have had to steal it if you had just given

it to me in the first place!" she snapped, wheeling around and pointing a finger in my direction. There was a deranged look in her purple eyes, and her teeth were gritted. "This was your fault! That man's blood is on your hands!"

My eyes widened as I stared at her. "I wouldn't sell you that book because it is so dangerous," I said.

"Of course it is," Silvia said. "That's why it belongs in spell weaver hands, and not just sitting around for some Ungifted to come and pick it up."

I glared at her across the mountaintop, and another gust of wind rushed around us, nearly knocking me off my feet.

"I'm sorry, new sister or whatever you might be, but I can't let you leave to go back and tell the police everything I just told you. It would sort of ruin the whole thing, wouldn't it? I just need to wait for things to calm down, go speak with the council, and I'll be home free – "

"Yeah, I don't think so," I said with a hollow laugh. "That's not happening. You aren't going anywhere unless you're in handcuffs."

Silvia snickered. "I'll give you credit for being brave, even if it's foolish. Do you really think you could take me on in a duel, young one? I have more years of experience using magic than you've been walking this earth. Do you know what that means? I will win."

My heart skipped a beat, and I swallowed nervously. She was right, but I couldn't let her know that.

Silvia, her eyes locked on mine, snapped her fingers. Another puff of purple smoke returned the red leather-bound book to her waiting arms.

"Now..." she said, flipping it open and paging through it. Even from this distance, I could see the pages glowing. The hum that I'd first heard when I opened the book filled my mind, as if calling me to read its secrets. "What spell would be best? A memory charm... Oh, what about a wind spell? No..." She flipped a few more pages.

My heart raced. If she actually managed to cast a spell, what chance did I have of surviving it?

*Use your power...*Athena said beside me.

I looked down at her, and she nodded her head up at me.

Use it.

"I could always use the same spell I used to kill poor old Burt, but that would be too obvious and we don't need two killings done the same way," Silvia said with a little chuckle. "Ah...here we are. This looks perfect."

My heartbeat thundered in my ears. I had to cross the distance between us. In order for my power to work, I had to touch her. And even then, I didn't know if it would work. Did I have to will my power into existence?

I took a deep breath and focused all of my thoughts on one thing: taking Silvia's power away. Survival was paramount, as was the safety of Faerywood Falls as a whole. If she was able to get away with murder, than things were only going to get worse from here.

"Yes, I like this," Silvia said, her eyes glued to the page.

Now was my chance.

In the same breath, the same heartbeat, Silvia opened her mouth to utter a spell at the very same second that I dashed across the distance between us, my hand outstretched to touch her. Even with just the very tips of my fingers. I knew that would be enough.

"*Li....son...shy....ren*"

The word had passed from her lips at the same second that my fingers just grazed the forearm that cradled the red tome.

"What are you doing?" she asked, stepping away from me in disgust, as if I were some sort of vile creature.

The spell was already forming as she stretched out her hand toward me. A brilliant ball of yellow light grew from the size of a golf ball to a softball in a matter of seconds. She smiled at me, her face bathed in the glow of the spell.

"See you on the other side..." she said, and the spell left her hand.

A surge of...something raced through my veins. It was almost the same feeling I'd gotten when I'd touched the woman at the gas station. But it was much, much stronger. Like a hurricane of magic through my body. I worried that I might burst.

I held my hand up directly at her, my eyes locked on hers. "*Lisonshyren*," I said calmly, steadily, and another ball of light appeared in my hand as hers hurtled toward me.

Mine swelled from a softball to the size of a watermelon, and turned blue like the hottest of flames.

I blinked, and released the spell.

It tore across the space between us at twice the speed as Silvia's spell. It collided with hers in midair, engulfing it, and continuing on as if nothing had happened.

Silvia's purple eyes grew wide as she gaped at me. "No... How did you – "

But her words were lost as the spell hit her square in the chest and sent her flying...straight off the cliff behind her and into the open air below.

18

W *ell...I can't say that I'm sorry to see her go.*

I wheeled around, a new voice I didn't recognize filling my mind. From the path back down the mountain, I saw a silvery wolf approaching, his golden eyes locked on mine.

My heart, already pounding so hard I worried I might pass out, skipped another beat.

Before my eyes, the wolf disappeared in a sudden, hazy mist and transformed into Lucan Valerio a moment later. He adjusted the navy blue tie he now wore, his golden eyes watching me closely. "Are you all right?"

"Yeah..." I said, staring up at him dumbfounded. "How did you – "

"I suppose you might say I've been keeping an eye on you," he said, a small, handsome smile appearing behind his beard. It disappeared quickly, though. "I heard everything that Silvia said. I must admit, I'm not surprised that she is the culprit. It's terrible what happened to Mr. Cassidy, and I'm glad, in a small sense, that he's been given the justice he deserved. I know it won't bring him back, but perhaps his spirit can rest easier."

I swallowed hard. "What do we do now?"

"Well, we will have to call the sheriff and inform him of Silvia's confession. He will have two testimonies, both yours and mine," Dr. Valerio said gently. He sighed. "I...think it would be best if we were to keep the magical aspects of this case a secret. The sheriff and many others in Faerywood Falls know nothing about us Gifted folks and the powers we possess, and it truly is best that it stay that way, as much as I dislike agreeing with the late spell weaver."

"So, what, we are going to lie?" I asked.

Dr. Valerio scratched at his beard. "There are times in which it is necessary."

I frowned. "I'm not sure that's true..."

"We will simply tell the sheriff that she admitted to killing the man over an unspecified personal grudge, and that she was so overcome with remorse that she threw herself from the cliff," he said.

"Why can't we tell him that she was the one who broke into the shop?" I asked.

"Oh, we certainly will tell him that," Dr. Valerio said. "But that will be for Mr. Cromwell's closure more than anything."

I made the emergency phone call on my cell. Then, we waited up there for the sheriff to arrive, as this area was now a crime scene and we would doubtless be wanted for questioning. All the while, I wasn't sure I was going to do as Dr. Valerio asked and keep the magical aspects of the case secret. They were the whole reason everything had happened in the first place.

Guilt racked me as I saw Sheriff Garland's car pull up on

the mountainside. There must have been some back trails I was unfamiliar with. I watched the sheriff slam his car door and labor the rest of the way uphill to where Lucan and I waited. Other cop cars pulled up and more police officers followed behind the sheriff.

"Marianne Huffler," Sheriff Garland said, panting a little as he reached the crest. "Why am I not surprised to find you in the middle of this? It seems you have the bad luck to stumble into violent situations quite a lot." His tone said he was wondering how much could be blamed on "bad luck" and how much might be credited to a meddlesome nature.

I bit my tongue while Lucan Valerio gave an explanation for what had happened here. His story sounded genuine, although I knew he must have carefully rehearsed it in his head during the long minutes while we had waited for the arrival of the police. He claimed I had come up here, suspecting Silvia Griffon of murder and theft, and confronted her. Knowing my plans and fearing for my safety, Dr. Valerio had followed me and arrived in time to witness Silvia's confession and sudden suicide.

To my great surprise, I found myself backing up Lucan Valerio's testimony. The whole truth was on the tip of my tongue but at the very last second, I decided that it was better to keep the magical aspects secret, as they involved me now, too.

Sheriff Garland questioned me briefly, while his men swarmed down a steep trail to retrieve the lifeless body of Silvia lying far below. I tried not to watch. Despite all that the spell weaver had done, it was a terrible way for anyone to die. Perhaps fearing I was too distressed to talk further, the sheriff allowed me to leave, saying we could finish our interview later.

"I can have someone drive you back to your cabin or to

your aunt's lodge," he said, not unkindly. A different cop might have resented my meddling in a murder case and my confrontation of a killer that had led to the murderer's death. But I got the sense Joe Garland was almost impressed by my courage.

"It's all right," I told him. "I need to walk off some nervous energy. I'll follow the trail down to where I parked."

"I'll walk with her," Lucan Valerio put in quickly. I sensed he was eager to hustle me away from the police before I said anything he wouldn't like.

But I didn't say anything more, even though as we walked away from the scene, I felt a stirring of guilt. I hated doing exactly what Silvia had done. She claimed she killed Burt to keep our secret. Was I no better than her for lying?

"You made the wise decision," Dr. Valerio told me as we started back toward the trail down the mountain with Athena following.

I stared back at him, setting aside my girlish attraction for a moment. "Honestly, I'm not sure what I am going to do about all this. The magical elements in Faerywood Falls, I mean. I've been dragged in without wanting to be, and look where it's gotten me."

Dr. Valerio nodded. "I understand. But how can you deny the calling in your soul, Marianne? Surely that would be too hard to ignore?"

My eyes narrowed. "I'm not entirely seduced by it, no. And I'm not entirely convinced that you or some other shifter aren't responsible for what's been happening to those hunters in the woods. Silvia insisted she wasn't responsible for that and I believe her. She had no motive for those deaths."

Dr. Valerio's gaze sharpened. "My faction has no involvement in that."

I pursed my lips. This wasn't the time to argue with him. "The fact that I told the sheriff the story you devised about the spell weaver's death doesn't mean that I'm on your side, Dr. Valerio. It doesn't mean that I'll permanently be keeping your secret and that of the other Gifted people in Faerywood Falls." Even though we were now out of sight of the police, I kept my voice low.

He smirked, and as the wind rustled his coppery hair, I found my heart skipping another beat. "Yes, well...after what I've seen of your own powerful abilities, it looks like the magic isn't just our secret anymore. It's yours, too."

And with that, Dr. Valerio inclined his head toward me with a warm smile on his face before dissolving into a cloud of hazy mist once more. A wolf appeared in his place, golden eyes gazing in my direction briefly before taking off into the darkening forest.

I watched him leave, my heart troubled.

Are you all right? Athena asked, nudging her nose against my calf muscles.

I blinked, clearing my mind. "Yeah, I think so..." I rubbed at my eyes, staring off through the trees at the now setting sun.

A breeze rushed through the trees, making my hair flutter out behind me.

We are always here...when you are ready to accept...who you are.

I inhaled deeply, the scent of the sweet pine and the coming rain. The rich earth beneath my feet was coating my shoes as I trekked down the trail.

The secret was mine, too...wasn't it? Mine to keep, mine to tell...mine to do with as I wanted.

Gifted. Magic. Faery.

These words had been fiction to me, and now they were my life. And what a life it was likely to be.

"Come on, Athena…" I said with a small smile down at my friend. "Let's go home."

Continue following the Mountain Magic Mysteries in Book 2: The Curious Curse of Faerywood Falls.

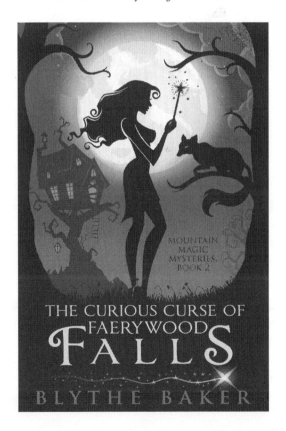

The air was growing warmer as the days passed. Spring was slowly giving way to summer. The days were longer, and the heat lingered longer in the air. The grass was thick on the ground, and the leaves were brilliant shades of brightest green.

I'd been in Faerywood Falls for some weeks now. Almost six, if my calendar was right. I was settled into my cabin. I knew I was settled because my sink was often filled with dishes and a layer of dust was starting to accumulate on my picture frames and the top of the small bookshelf I'd brought home from the antique shop one afternoon. It was a good reminder to get back on a cleaning routine.

I found myself longing to sit out on the tiny front porch of the lakeside cabin I'd taken residence in. I never thought I'd like living in such a small space, but the reality was it was perfect for one person. And since I spent a lot of time working at the antique shop or hanging out up at the lodge with my aunt and cousin, I didn't need a ton of space.

My fox companion. Athena, on the other hand, would beg to differ. What she wanted more than anything were more windows to let the sunlight in. On my days off, she'd stretch out, making herself as long as she could, exposing her belly to the warm light. I'd asked if she wanted me to get her a bed that was just her size to sleep in, but she refused. She'd much rather curl up at the foot of my bed with me. She said it was because human beds were more comfortable, and I would just smile, knowing that what she really liked was being near me and sharing in some body heat.

She was good at staying out of sight. People might question why I kept a fox as a pet, especially those who had no idea about the magical gifts that gave me the ability to actually speak with her. The gift wasn't mine, originally. I'd accidentally stolen it from some kind-faced woman working at a gas station on the outskirts of town. That was what I could do as a faery: borrow the powers of others.

It was another thing not a lot of people knew about me. Until I moved to Faerywood Falls, I'd had no idea, either. I was the first faery born in these parts in a long, long time. Those who were Gifted, or possessed some kind of magical or mystical powers, would likely vie for my support if they were to find out. That, or they'd try to take advantage of my abilities, most of which I hardly understood how to use yet. In a lot of ways, I was still trying to come to terms with the truth of my existence. All I knew was that my adopted mother found me just outside the forest when I was an infant. Nothing was known about me or my biological family aside from a letter left with me in my basket; it warned anyone who found me not to take me away from Faerywood Falls, or a curse would befall me.

And it had. Until I had finally returned to this place again, where the magic in my blood called me.

There were a lot of people who didn't know that magic even existed in Faerywood Falls. People like Abe Cromwell, the man I worked for. His little antique shop was of great interest to many Gifted in the area, as sometimes magical items would pass through without his detection. The longer I worked there, the more I became convinced that they were the sole reason why his business hadn't gone under. Those customers paid handsomely, telling old Abe that the pieces they sought were incredibly valuable. He never questioned it, and lived blissfully unaware of the magical abilities of those who passed in and out of his shop.

Dr. Valerio was one such patron. As handsome as he was mysterious, he would come to the shop looking for various items twice a week, at least. His golden eyes were hard to look away from, and I couldn't tell if it was because of my subtle attraction to him, or the fact that I knew he was, in fact, a werewolf, and the leader of all the lycanthropes in Faerywood Falls.

Another frequent shopper was Cain Blackburn. He'd only ever been able to come on days when the shop was open past dark. The town believed the Blackburns to be a very wealthy family, whose riches were passed from one generation to the next. The truth was, however, that Cain Blackburn and the rest of his "family" were vampires and had been living in the same castle since arriving in the valley several centuries before.

Faerywood Falls never failed to enchant me, and the more I learned about it, the more I'd grown to love it.

It was one evening in early June that Dr. Valerio came in for yet another visit that week. He'd purchased a set of crystal decanters from Mr. Cromwell, three of them, and was waiting on a delivery of a fourth. He'd told me in private that they were almost four hundred years old and had been made with liquid moonlight. I wasn't sure if he was being completely honest with me, but after everything I'd seen in my short time there, I wouldn't have been surprised.

After he was gone, the last two customers of the day also left the store, carrying their bags of very non-magical wooden bookends. They waved to me as the little bell over the door chimed at their departure.

"Another day done, eh, Marianne?"

I turned and saw Mr. Cromwell standing in the doorway up to his apartment above the store. He smiled at me, the wrinkles near his eyes prominent in the golden light of the setting sun.

I returned his smile easily as I wiped down the back counter. "Yes, it is," I said. "You'll be pleased to hear that the Robinson's came and purchased that 19th century table."

"They decided they wanted it after all?" Mr. Cromwell asked, hobbling into the store. It hurt my heart to see his limp getting worse. Aunt Candace had offered to take him to the doctor, but he refused every time. He knew it was age, and there was nothing to be done about that.

Not for the first time, I wondered if the magical book that Silvia Griffin had stolen would have a spell in it to help him. If only I knew where the book actually was...

"They also purchased the chairs with it, and that nice credenza we put out yesterday," I said, checking the cash register.

"Very good," he said. "Are they coming by tomorrow to pick it up?"

"That's the plan," I said.

"I feel terrible that Dr. Valerio's decanter hasn't come in yet," Mr. Cromwell said.

"He said he understood and that he'd just swing by tomorrow after work to check again."

"He's such a patient man," Mr. Cromwell said. "We're

fortunate to have men like him and Mr. Blackburn residing in our small town."

"I think you're right," I said.

Some of the hairs on my arms stood on end, but all in all, I did agree with him. They were interesting men, both in the human world and in the magical one. They had great influence. And while they didn't always get along, I wanted to believe that they both had the best interests at heart for Faerywood Falls as a whole.

"Well, you've been here a long time today," Mr. Cromwell said. "I appreciate you coming in early to help me take inventory. With the summer upon us, we should expect more customers, and I just want to make sure we're ready for them."

"Oh, don't worry, we will be," I said.

"Very good," he said with a smile. "Now, off you go. I'm sure you want to enjoy what little of today you have left."

"And you should get some rest, too, Mr. Cromwell," I said. "Like you said, summer's coming, and you should give yourself time to enjoy all that warm sun."

He grinned. "I do enjoy a good lie down in the sun..."

I bid him goodbye from the back of my bike as I headed off into the darkening street. The sun had just dipped below the horizon and the sky above was painted in bright pinks and oranges and grays. I wanted to look up at the clouds more than the road ahead of me, but I promised myself a nice cup of tea while I sat on my porch, hoping that I'd get a chance to catch the last of the light as the day gave way to the starry night.

My backpack rustled on my back, and as soon as we were out of sight of the shop, Athena appeared, shaking her tiny, copper head, her black nose sniffing the air frantically.

Her lips parted and she began to pant in the warm evening air.

I think we need to invest in a mesh backpack, she informed me. *It's starting to get a little warm in here.*

"I bet it is," I said. "Alright, I'll see if I can find anything online tonight. But we've gotta be smart. I don't want Mr. Cromwell finding you."

Don't worry so much, she said. *I always hear him coming before he's anywhere near us.*

We rode along for a while, cars passing by us on the road, their headlights banishing the shadows in their paths. The streetlights were flickering to life, their warm glow preparing for night's long embrace.

Downtown was quiet, which wasn't a huge surprise in the middle of the week. The shops had all closed up for the night already and the only place that still had their lights on was the restaurant on the corner.

"I think Mr. Cromwell's right," I said. "There are definitely more people around now."

Tourist season has begun, Athena said.

We crested a hill, about two miles from the lake where our cabin was. A long stretch of fields ran alongside the road to our left. Beside us, a long wrought iron fence appeared behind a thick cluster of trees.

We passed by it every day. The Faerywood Falls cemetery. It rested on a beautiful stretch of land, with rolling hills and large, full trees scattered throughout. Even from a distance, it was easy to see that many of the tombstones were old, especially those closest to the entrance. Some days, Athena and I liked to see what names we could glimpse through the fence.

Not for the first time, I wondered if poor Burt Cassidy was buried in there. It hadn't been all that long since I'd found out the truth about his murder, and yet, it felt like it happened ages ago. Life in Faerywood Falls had kind of gone back to some sense of normal...as normal as it ever was, most likely.

So, what are we having for dinner tonight –

Athena's words were pushed from my mind when a scream, high pitched and terrified, echoed through the cemetery beside us.

My hands yanked on the brakes, the tires skidding to a halt on the graveled sidewalk.

"What was that?" I asked, my heart pounding in my ears.

I don't know, Athena said. Her front paws were perched on my shoulder, and her nose was pointed up into the air, sniffing madly.

"Did it come from in there?" I asked, pointing through the wrought iron bars of the fence into the cemetery.

I think it did.

I swallowed hard, my throat tight. I spun my bike around and pointed it back toward the main entrance, which we'd passed a few moments before. "We should go see. Someone might need our help."

Shouldn't we call someone for help instead? Athena asked. *You don't know what we could be walking into.*

But I ignored her as I put my feet on the pedals and made my way toward the gate.

My ears strained as I turned my bike onto the dirt drive leading into the cemetery. Where had the scream come from?

"Whoever it was, they sounded terrified," I said as I pushed myself further and further into the darkening cemetery. There weren't nearly as many lights in here, and all of the headstones cast long, eerie shadows across the patches of grass.

Which is why I was warning you against coming in here in the first place, Athena said. *We have no idea what could have frightened them so much.*

Her words made sense, but my legs kept pumping and my eyes kept scanning. I had no idea what sort of disconnect was happening in my brain, as I was terrified of what I might find, yet curiosity and determination kept pushing me onward. I had no idea where the courage came from, but I knew I couldn't turn back now.

We made a hard right turn. I was starting to lose faith that we'd ever find the screamer. It was getting darker by the minute, and the cemetery was huge. She could've been anywhere.

"Maybe I should call Dr. Valerio..." I said. "He'd be able to get his wolves in here, right? They wouldn't be afraid of the dark."

Dr. Valerio might have some sort of interest in you, but I don't think he'd drop everything to come at your beck and call, Athena said.

I sighed, squinting into the darkness. She was probably right, though I liked the idea of being able to pass something like this off to someone with a lot more power than I had.

Then again, I supposed the police were only a phone call away, if necessary...

There, Athena said. *Something's different on the air.*

I turned my bike in the direction her nose pointed, and headed between a row of tombstones.

My tires bounced along on the uneven dirt, and I grimaced as I realized exactly what I was doing.

"I'm sorry, I'm sorry," I said as we passed over grave after grave. I couldn't imagine this was a good way to earn myself any friends in Faerywood Falls, especially among those who were able to talk to the ghosts.

It was so dark that I stopped the bike, pulled out my phone, and turned on its flashlight. I continued on, following the narrow beam of light and Athena's nose, bumping along through the dark.

It's close, Athena said. *Slow down –*

But I'd already stopped the bike. Just at the end of the flashlight from my phone, the body of a young woman lay sprawled across the grass, her glassy, lifeless eyes staring right at me.

END OF EXCERPT

ABOUT THE AUTHOR

Blythe Baker is a thirty-something bottle redhead from the South Central part of the country. When she's not slinging words and creating new worlds and characters, she's acting as chauffeur to her children and head groomer to her household of beloved pets.

Blythe enjoys long walks with her dog on sweaty days, grubbing in her flower garden, cooking, and ruthlessly de-cluttering her overcrowded home. She also likes binge-watching mystery shows on TV and burying herself in books about murder.

To learn more about Blythe, visit her website and sign up for her newsletter at www.blythebaker.com

Made in the USA
Middletown, DE
16 May 2019